SCIENTIFIC AMERICAN EXPLORES BIG IDEAS

The Search for Extraterrestrial Intelligence

The Editors of *Scientific American*

SCIENTIFIC AMERICAN EDUCATIONAL PUBLISHING

New York

Published in 2023 by Scientific American Educational Publishing
in association with **The Rosen Publishing Group**
2544 Clinton Street, Buffalo NY 14224

Contains material from Scientific American®, a division of Springer Nature America, Inc., reprinted by permission as well as original material from Rosen Publishing Group®.

First Edition

Scientific American
Lisa Pallatroni: Custom Book Editor

Rosen Publishing
Daniel R. Faust: Compiling Editor
Michael Moy: Senior Graphic Designer

Cataloging-in-Publication Data
Names: Scientific American.
Title: The Search for extraterrestrial intelligence / Scientific American.
Description: New York : Scientific American Educational, 2023. | Series: Scientific american explores big ideas| Includes bibliographic information, glossary and index.
Identifiers: ISBN 9781684169481 (pbk) | ISBN 9781684169498 (library bound) | ISBN 9781684169504 (ebook)
Subjects: LCSH: Extraterrestrial beings– Juvenile literature | Extraterrestrial life – Juvenile literature | Universe– Juvenile literature
Classification: LCC QB54 S35 2023 | DDC 576.8/39 –dc23

Manufactured in the United States of America
Websites listed were live at the time of publication.

Cover: ktsdesign/Shutterstock.com

CPSIA Compliance Information: Batch #SACW23.
For further information, contact Rosen Publishing at 1-800-237-9932.

CONTENTS

INTRODUCTION

Are we alone in the universe? It's a question that scientists and philosophers have pondered for the entirety of human history. What had once simply been a philosophical debate has, with the scientific advances of the 20th and 21st centuries, become a true scientific investigation. In the March 1955 issue of *Scientific American*, John D. Krauss proposed using radio telescopes to scan the cosmos for signals from alien civilizations. In 1960, the first modern search for extraterrestrial intelligence (or SETI) began at the Greenbank Observatory in West Virginia. Numerous SETI projects continued to operate all over the world, some funded by government organizations like NASA and others funded by private citizens.

The articles presented in this volume attempt to answer a few basic questions with regards to humanity's search for extraterrestrial intelligence. What many people probably write off as the stuff of science fiction is, in fact, an ongoing scientific pursuit. Section 1, "The Origin of Life," asks the fundamental question: What is life and when did it begin? More specifically, how and when did life begin? Is life unique to our planet, or can it be found elsewhere in the universe? Section 2, "Searching for Signs of Life," details some of the ways that scientists are searching for life beyond the confines of Earth, whether it be located elsewhere in our solar system or on some distant exoplanet. Section 3, "Are We Alone?" examines the possibilities that there could be other intelligent life in the universe and that it might be searching for us while we are searching for it. And, finally, Section 4, "Making Contact," offers suggestions about how we should proceed in the event that we finally do make contact with an extraterrestrial intelligence–or it makes contact with us.

Section 1: The Origin of Life

When Did Life Start in the Universe?

By Avi Loeb

Our sun is not a typical star. Most stars are one-10th as massive and will live hundreds of times longer than the sun. Moreover, most stars formed billions of years before the sun, based on the observed star formation history since the big bang.

Why were we born so late in cosmic history around a relatively massive star like the sun? Statistically speaking, we were more likely to exist earlier or around a lower-mass star.

The Copernican principle asserts that we are not privileged observers of our universe. It stems from the discovery made half a millennium ago by Nicolaus Copernicus that we are not located at the physical center of the cosmos as thought previously. If this mediocrity principle applies to all of our cosmic circumstances, then there must be physical reasons for why our particular form of intelligent life did not arise around an early or dwarf star.

Two obvious explanations come to mind. First, the material that assembled to make early stars lacked the heavy elements that are essential for life as we know it. This includes the heavy elements that make rocky planets like Earth, as well as the oxygen and carbon needed for water-based organic chemistry.

Second, dwarf stars are fainter, bringing their habitable zone closer in. Given this proximity, Earth-like planets would have their atmosphere stripped by stellar winds or their surface sterilized by UV flares from these dwarf stars.

Nevertheless, many sunlike stars with a similar heavy element abundance must have formed long before the sun because we see the products of their death as white dwarfs. It is therefore difficult to imagine that we are the first advanced civilization to appear on the cosmic scene. Can we find evidence for earlier participants in the cosmic story of life?

One approach is to search for signatures of life around older stars in our Milky Way galaxy. The search could target biosignatures, such as oxygen and methane in the atmospheres of planets around them, or technosignatures, such as radio or laser transmission, industrial pollution, or city lights.

A second method is to search for early technological civilizations that produced powerful beacons of light or transformed their environment in ways that are detectable across cosmological distances. For the fingerprints to be visible over the vast universe requires them to possess tremendous advances relative to our technological capabilities, as we are still struggling to harvest a tiny fraction of the solar power intercepted by Earth.

The third and simplest way is to search within our solar system for technological packages that were shipped to interstellar space by advanced civilizations billions of years ago.

For example, the Perseverance rover could bump into the wreckage of such objects on the surface of Mars. We could also search our moon, which (in a way) serves as a museum for collecting ancient artifacts that have crashed into it over time, because it lacks an atmosphere that would burn them up before impact and has no geological activity that would mix them with its interior after impact.

In total, we should explore early cosmic life in all possible ways to recognize who (if anyone) predated us and what can we learn from them.

The ancient Greek culture during the time of Homer, the reputed author of the *Iliad* and *Odyssey*, valued hospitality to new guests. So much so that the Greek god Zeus was also called Zeus Xenios in his role as a protector of strangers. The concept of xenia reflected the kindness of hospitality.

The ritualized friendship to guests by the ancient Greeks was beneficial, as it enabled them to access new information from visitors who arrived at their doorstep from distant territories. Today, one might regard this motivation as outdated because of the easy flow of information across Earth through the internet, through global trade, and through air travel. However, the flow of information about life across interstellar space is currently lacking–at least, it is for us. In that context, we should follow the ancient Greeks and endorse the notion of xenia with a modern twist.

The idea of interstellar xenia suggests that we should welcome all visitors–even if they arrive in the form of old hardware with artificial rather than natural intelligence–that could carry valuable information from earlier times. Our current technological civilization could benefit greatly from the knowledge it might garner from such encounters. After all, we share the same cosmic neighborhood as these cosmic visitors do.

On a recent breezy evening, I noticed an unfamiliar visitor standing in front of my home and asked for his identity. He explained that he used to live in my home half a century ago. I welcomed him to our backyard where he noted that his father buried their cat and placed a tombstone engraved with its name. We went there and found the tombstone.

Our galactic neighborhood could have been visited many times by passing visitors over the past 10 billion years. To find them, we need to monitor the sky and search for unfamiliar objects near our home planet. This is precisely the rationale behind the recently announced Galileo Project, which aims to identify the nature of unusual interstellar objects in the vicinity of Earth.

If we find old visitors, they might provide us with a new perspective about the history of life in our cosmic neighborhood. In so doing, they would bring a deeper meaning to our own life within the keen historic friendship that we owe them in our shared space.

Interstellar xenia might be the key to the prosperity of our culture, just as it led to the intellectual richness of the ancient Greek philosophy and literature.

About the Author

Avi Loeb is former chair (2011-2020) of the astronomy department at Harvard University, founding director of Harvard's Black Hole Initiative and director of the Institute for Theory and Computation at the Harvard-Smithsonian Center for Astrophysics. He also chairs the Board on Physics and Astronomy of the National Academies and the advisory board for the Breakthrough Starshot project, and is a member of President's Council of Advisors on Science and Technology. Loeb is the bestselling author of Extraterrestrial: The First Sign of Intelligent Life Beyond Earth *(Houghton Mifflin Harcourt).*

Did Life Come from Another World?

By David Warmflash and Benjamin Weiss

Most scientists have long assumed that life on Earth is a homegrown phenomenon. According to the conventional hypothesis, the earliest living cells emerged as a result of chemical evolution on our planet billions of years ago in a process called abiogenesis. The alternative possibility–that living cells or their precursors arrived from space–strikes many people as science fiction. Developments over the past decade, however, have given new credibility to the idea that Earth's biosphere could have arisen from an extraterrestrial seed.

Planetary scientists have learned that early in its history, our solar system could have included many worlds with liquid water, the essential ingredient for life as we know it. Recent data from NASA's Mars exploration rovers corroborate previous suspicions that water has at least intermittently flowed on the Red Planet in the past. It is not unreasonable to hypothesize that life existed on Mars long ago and perhaps continues there. Life may have also evolved on Europa, Jupiter's fourth–largest moon, which appears to possess liquid water under its icy surface. Saturn's biggest satellite, Titan, is rich in organic compounds; given the moon's frigid temperatures, it would be highly surprising to find living forms there, but they cannot be ruled out. Life may have even gained a toehold on torrid Venus. The Venusian surface is probably too hot and under too much atmospheric pressure to be habitable, but the planet could conceivably support microbial life high in its atmosphere. And, most likely, the surface conditions on Venus were not always so harsh. Venus may have once been similar to early Earth.

Moreover, the expanses of interplanetary space are not the forbidding barrier they once seemed. Over the past 20 years scientists have determined that more than 30 meteorites found on Earth originally came from the Martian crust, based on the composition of gases trapped within some of the rocks. Meanwhile biologists have discovered organisms durable enough to survive at least a short journey inside such meteorites. Although no one is suggesting that these particular organisms actually made the trip, they serve as a proof of principle. It is not implausible that life could have arisen on Mars and then come to Earth, or the reverse. Researchers are now intently studying the transport of biological materials between planets to get a better sense of whether it ever occurred. This effort may shed light on some of modern science's most compelling questions: Where and how did life originate? Are radically different forms of life possible? And how common is life in the universe?

From Philosophy to the Laboratory

To the ancient philosophers, the creation of life from nonliving matter seemed so magical, so much the realm of the gods, that some actually preferred the idea that ready–made living forms had come to Earth from elsewhere. Anaxagoras, a Greek philosopher who lived 2,500 years ago, proposed a hypothesis called "panspermia" (Greek for "all seeds"), which posited that all life, and indeed all things, originated from the combination of tiny seeds pervading the cosmos. In modern times, several leading scientists–including British physicist Lord Kelvin, Swedish chemist Svante Arrhenius, and Francis Crick, co–discoverer of the structure of DNA–have advocated various conceptions of panspermia. To be sure, the idea has also had less reputable proponents, but they should not detract from the fact that panspermia is a serious hypothesis, a potential phenomenon that we should not ignore when considering the distribution and evolution of life in the universe and how life came to exist specifically on Earth.

Earth's biosphere could have arisen from an extraterrestrial seed.

In its modern form, the panspermia hypothesis addresses how biological material might have arrived on our planet but not how life originated in the first place. No matter where it started, life had to arise from nonliving matter. Abiogenesis moved from the realm of philosophy to that of experimentation in the 1950s, when chemists Stanley L. Miller and Harold C. Urey of the University of Chicago demonstrated that amino acids and other molecules important to life could be generated from simple compounds believed to exist on early Earth. It is now thought that molecules of ribonucleic acid (RNA) could have also assembled from smaller compounds and played a vital role in the development of life.

In present–day cells, specialized RNA molecules help to build proteins. Some RNAs act as messengers between the genes, which are made of deoxyribonucleic acid (DNA), and the ribosomes, the protein factories of the cell. Other RNAs bring amino acids–the building blocks of proteins–to the ribosomes, which in turn contain yet another type of RNA. The RNAs work in concert with protein enzymes that aid in linking the amino acids together, but researchers have found that the RNAs in the ribosome can perform the crucial step of protein synthesis alone. In the early stages of life's evolution, all the enzymes may have been RNAs, not proteins. Because RNA enzymes could have manufactured the first proteins without the need for preexisting protein enzymes to initiate the process, abiogenesis is not the chicken–and–egg problem that it was once thought to be. A prebiotic system of RNAs and proteins could have gradually developed the ability to replicate its molecular parts, crudely at first but then ever more efficiently.

This new understanding of life's origins has transformed the scientific debate over panspermia. It is no longer an either–or question of whether the first microbes arose on Earth or arrived from space. In the chaotic early history of the solar system, our planet was subject to intense bombardment by meteorites containing simple organic compounds. The young Earth could have also received more complex molecules with enzymatic functions, molecules that were prebiotic but part of a system that was already well on its way to biology. After landing in a suitable habitat on our planet, these molecules could have continued their evolution to living cells. In other words, an intermediate scenario is possible: life could have roots both on Earth and in space. But which steps in the development of life occurred where? And once life took hold, how far did it spread?

Scientists who study panspermia used to concentrate only on assessing the basic plausibility of the idea, but they have recently sought to estimate the probability that biological materials made the journey to Earth from other planets or moons. To begin their interplanetary trip, the materials would have to be ejected from their planet of origin into space by the impact of a comet or asteroid. While traveling through space, the ejected rocks or dust particles would need to be captured by the gravity of another planet or moon, then decelerated enough to fall to the surface, passing through the atmosphere if one were present. Such transfers happen frequently throughout the solar system, although it is easier for ejected material to travel from bodies more distant from the sun to those closer in and easier for materials to end up on a more massive body. Indeed, dynamic simulations by University of British Columbia astrophysicist Brett Gladman suggest that the mass transferred from Earth to Mars is only a few percent of that delivered from Mars to Earth. For this reason, the most commonly discussed panspermia scenario involves the transport of microbes or their precursors from Mars to Earth.

Simulations of asteroid or comet impacts on Mars indicate that materials can be launched into a wide variety of orbits. Gladman and his colleagues have estimated that every few million years Mars undergoes an impact powerful enough to eject rocks that could eventually reach Earth. The interplanetary journey is usually a long one: most of the approximately one ton of Martian ejecta that lands on Earth every year has spent several million years in space. But a tiny percentage of the Martian rocks arriving on Earth's surface–about one out of every 10 million–will have spent less than a year in space. Within three years of the impact event, about 10 fist–size rocks weighing more than 100 grams complete the voyage from

Mars to Earth. Smaller debris, such as pebble–size rocks and dust particles, are even more likely to make a quick trip between planets; very large rocks do so much less frequently.

Could biological entities survive this journey? First, let us consider whether microorganisms could live through the ejection process from the meteorite's parent body. Recent laboratory impact experiments have found that certain strains of bacteria can survive the accelerations and jerks (rates of changes of acceleration) that would be encountered during a typical high–pressure ejection from Mars. It is crucial, however, that the impact and ejection do not heat the meteorites enough to destroy the biological materials within them.

Planetary geologists formerly believed that any impact ejecta with speeds exceeding the Martian escape velocity would almost certainly be vaporized or at least completely melted. This idea was later discounted, though, following the discovery of unmelted, largely intact meteorites from the moon and Mars. These findings led H. Jay Melosh of the University of Arizona to calculate that a small percentage of ejected rocks could indeed be catapulted from Mars via impact without any heating at all. In short, Melosh proposed that when the upward–propagating pressure wave resulting from an impact reaches the planetary surface, it undergoes a 180–degree phase change that nearly cancels the pressure within a thin layer of rock just below the surface. Because this "spall zone" experiences very little compression while the layers below are put under enormous pressure, rocks near the surface can be ejected relatively undeformed at high speeds.

Next, let us consider survivability during the entry into Earth's atmosphere. Edward Anders, formerly of the Enrico Fermi Institute at the the University of Chicago, has shown that interplanetary dust particles decelerate gently in Earth's upper atmosphere, thus avoiding heating. Meteorites, in contrast, experience significant friction, so their surfaces typically melt during atmospheric passage. The heat pulse, however, has time to travel a few millimeters at most into the meteorite's interior, so organisms buried deep in the rock would certainly survive.

Over the past five years a series of papers by one of us (Weiss) and his colleagues analyzed two types of Martian meteorites: the nakhlites, a set of rocks blasted off Mars by an asteroid or comet impact 11 million years ago, and ALH84001, which left the Red Planet four million years earlier. (ALH84001 became famous in 1996 when a group of scientists led by David McKay of the NASA Johnson Space Center claimed that the rock showed traces of fossilized microorganisms akin to Earth's bacteria; a decade later researchers are still debating whether the meteorite contains evidence of Martian life.) By studying the magnetic properties of the meteorites and the composition of the gases trapped within them, Weiss and his collaborators found that ALH84001 and at least two of the seven nakhlites discovered so far were not heated more than a few hundred degrees Celsius since they were part of the Martian surface. Furthermore, the fact that the nakhlites are nearly pristine rocks, untouched by high–pressure shock waves, implies that the Martian impact did not heat them above 100 degrees C.

Many, though not all, terrestrial prokaryotes (simple one–celled organisms such as bacteria that lack a membrane–bound nucleus) and eukaryotes (organisms with well–defined nuclei) could survive this temperature range. This result was the first direct experimental evidence that material could travel from planet to planet without being thermally sterilized at any point from ejection to landing.

The Problem of Radiation

For panspermia to occur, however, microorganisms need to survive not only ejection from the first planet and atmospheric entry to the second but the interplanetary voyage itself. Life–bearing meteoroids and dust particles would be exposed to the vacuum of space, extremes in temperature, and several different kinds of radiation. Of particular concern is the sun's high–energy ultraviolet (UV) light, which breaks the bonds that hold together the carbon atoms of organic molecules. It is very easy to shield against UV, though; just a few millionths of a meter of opaque material is enough to protect bacteria.

Indeed, a European study using NASA's Long Duration Exposure Facility (LDEF), a satellite deployed by the space shuttle in 1984 and retrieved from orbit by the shuttle six years later, showed that a thin aluminum cover afforded adequate UV shielding to spores of the bacterial species *Bacillus subtilis*. Of the spores protected by the aluminum but exposed to the vacuum and temperature extremes of space, 80 percent remained viable–researchers reanimated them into active bacterial cells at the end of the mission. As for the spores not covered by aluminum and therefore directly exposed to solar UV radiation, most were destroyed, but not all. About one in 10,000 unshielded spores stayed viable, and the presence of substances such as glucose and salts increased their survival rates. Even within an object as small as a dust particle, solar UV would not necessarily render an entire microbial colony sterile. And if the colony were inside something as large as a pebble, UV protection would be sharply increased.

Informative as it was, the LDEF study was conducted in low Earth orbit, well within our planet's protective magnetic field. Thus, this research could not say much about the effects of interplanetary charged particles, which cannot penetrate Earth's magnetosphere. From time to time, the sun produces bursts of energetic ions and electrons; furthermore, charged particles are a major component of the galactic cosmic radiation that constantly bombards our solar system. Protecting living things from charged particles, as well as from high–energy radiation such as gamma rays, is trickier than shielding against UV. A layer of rock just a few microns thick blocks UV, but adding more shielding actually increases the dose of other types of radiation. The reason is that charged particles and high–energy photons interact with the rocky shielding material, producing showers of secondary radiation within the meteorite.

These showers could reach any microbes inside the rock unless it was very big, about two meters or more in diameter. As we have noted above, though, large rocks make fast interplanetary voyages very infrequently. Consequently, in addition to UV protection, what really matters is how resistant a microbe is to all components of space radiation and how quickly the life–bearing meteorite moves from planet to planet. The shorter the journey, the lower the total radiation dose and hence the greater the chance of survival.

In fact, *B. subtilis* is fairly robust in terms of its radiation resistance. Even more hardy is *Deinococcus radiodurans*, a bacterial species that was discovered during the 1950s by agricultural scientist Arthur W. Anderson. This organism survives radiation doses given to sterilize food products and even thrives inside nuclear reactors. The same cellular mechanisms that help *D. radiodurans* repair its DNA, build extra–thick cell walls, and otherwise protect itself from radiation also mitigate damage from dehydration. Theoretically, if organisms with such capabilities were embedded within material catapulted from Mars the way that the nakhlites and ALH84001 apparently were (that is, without excessive heating), some fraction of the organisms would still be viable after many years, perhaps several decades, in interplanetary space.

Yet the actual long–term survival of active organisms, spores or complex organic molecules beyond Earth's magnetosphere has never been tested. Such experiments, which would put the biological materials within simulated meteoritic materials and expose them to the environment of interplanetary space, could be conducted on the surface of the moon. In fact, biological samples were carried onboard the Apollo lunar missions as part of an early incarnation of the European radiation study. The longest Apollo mission, though, lasted no more than 12 days, and samples were kept within the Apollo spacecraft and thus not exposed to the full space–radiation environment. In the future, scientists could place experimental packages on the lunar surface or on interplanetary trajectories for several years before returning them to Earth for laboratory analysis. Researchers are currently considering these approaches.

Meanwhile a long–term study known as the Martian Radiation Environment Experiment (MARIE) is under way. Launched by NASA in 2001 as part of the Mars *Odyssey* orbiter, MARIE's instruments are measuring doses of galactic cosmic rays and energetic solar particles as the spacecraft circles the Red Planet. Although MARIE includes no biological material, its sensors are designed to focus on the range of space radiation that is most harmful to DNA.

Future Studies

As we have shown, panspermia is plausible theoretically. But in addition, important aspects of the hypothesis have made the transition from plausibility to quantitative science. Meteorite evidence shows that material has been transferred between planets throughout the history of the solar system and that this process still occurs at a well–established rate. Furthermore, laboratory studies have demonstrated that a sizable fraction of microorganisms within a piece of planetary material ejected from a Mars–size planet could survive ejection into space and entry through Earth's atmosphere. But other parts of the panspermia hypothesis are harder to pin down. Investigators need more data to determine whether radiation–resistant organisms such as *B. subtilis* or *D. radiodurans* could live through an interplanetary journey. And even this research would not reveal the likelihood that it actually happened in the case of Earth's biosphere, because the studies involve present–day terrestrial life–forms; the organisms living billions of years ago could have fared much worse or much better.

Moreover, scientists cannot quantify the likelihood that life exists or once existed on planets other than Earth. Researchers simply do not know enough about the origin of any system of life, including that of Earth, to draw solid conclusions about the probability of abiogenesis occurring on any particular world. Given suitable ingredients and conditions, perhaps life needs hundreds of millions of years to get started. Or perhaps five minutes is enough. All we can say with any certainty is that by 2.7 billion years ago, or perhaps several hundred million years earlier, life–forms were thriving on Earth.

Because it is not possible at this time to quantify all the steps of the panspermia scenario, investigators cannot estimate how much biological material or how many living cells most likely arrived at

Earth's surface in a given period. Moreover, the transfer of viable organisms does not automatically imply the successful seeding of the planet that receives them, particularly if the planet already has life. If, for example, Martian microbes arrived on Earth after life independently arose on our planet, the extraterrestrial organisms may not have been able to replace or coexist with the homegrown species. It is also conceivable that Martian life did find a suitable niche on Earth but that scientists have simply not identified it yet. Researchers have inventoried no more than a few percent of the total number of bacterial species on this planet. Groups of organisms that are genetically unrelated to the known life on Earth might exist unrecognized right under our noses.

Ultimately, scientists may not be able to know whether and to what extent panspermia has occurred until they discover life on another planet or moon. For example, if future space missions find life on the Red Planet and report that Martian biochemistry is very different from our own, researchers would know immediately that life on Earth did not come from Mars. If the biochemistries were similar, however, scientists might begin to wonder if perhaps the two biospheres had a common origin. Assuming that Martian life–forms used DNA to store genetic information, investigators could study the nucleotide sequences to settle the question. If the Martian DNA sequences did not follow the same genetic code used by living cells on Earth to make proteins, researchers would conclude that Mars–Earth panspermia is doubtful. But many other scenarios are possible. Investigators might find that Martian life uses RNA or something else entirely to guide its replication. Indeed, yet–to–be–discovered organisms on Earth may fall into this category as well, and the exotic terrestrial creatures might turn out to be related to the Martian life–forms.

Whether terrestrial life emerged on Earth or through biological seeding from space or as the result of some intermediate scenario, the answer would be meaningful. The confirmation of Mars–Earth panspermia would suggest that life, once started, could readily spread within a star system. If, on the other hand, researchers find evidence of Martian organisms that emerged independently of terrestrial life, it would suggest that abiogenesis can occur with ease throughout the cosmos. What is more, biologists would be able to compare Earth organisms with alien forms and develop a more general definition of life. We would finally begin to understand the laws of biology the way we understand the laws of chemistry and physics—as fundamental properties of nature.

About the Authors

David Warmflash and Benjamin Weiss have taken different yet complementary approaches to studying whether life could have come to Earth from another world. Warmflash is an astrobiologist at the University of Houston and the NASA Johnson Space Center. He is currently helping to develop molecular tests to search for microorganisms on Mars and the Jovian moon Europa. Weiss is assistant professor of planetary sciences at the Massachusetts Institute of Technology. His recent studies of various Martian meteorites suggest that they were not heat–sterilized during their transfer from Mars to Earth.

The Origin of Life on Earth

By Alonso Ricardo, Jack W. Szostak

Every living cell, even the simplest bacterium, teems with molecular contraptions that would be the envy of any nanotechnologist. As they incessantly shake or spin or crawl around the cell, these machines cut, paste, and copy genetic molecules, shuttle nutrients around or turn them into energy, build and repair cellular membranes, relay mechanical, chemical, or electrical messages–the list goes on and on, and new discoveries add to it all the time.

It is virtually impossible to imagine how a cell's machines, which are mostly protein-based catalysts called enzymes, could have formed spontaneously as life first arose from nonliving matter around 3.7 billion years ago. To be sure, under the right conditions some building blocks of proteins, the amino acids, form easily from simpler chemicals, as Stanley L. Miller and Harold C. Urey of the University of Chicago discovered in pioneering experiments in the 1950s. But going from there to proteins and enzymes is a different matter.

A cell's protein-making process involves complex enzymes pulling apart the strands of DNA's double helix to extract the information contained in genes (the blueprints for the proteins) and translate it into the finished product. Thus, explaining how life began entails a serious paradox: it seems that it takes proteins–as well as the information now stored in DNA–to make proteins.

On the other hand, the paradox would disappear if the first organisms did not require proteins at all. Recent experiments suggest it would have been possible for genetic molecules similar to DNA or to its close relative RNA to form spontaneously. And because these molecules can curl up in different shapes and act as rudimentary catalysts, they may have become able to copy themselves–to reproduce–without the need for proteins. The earliest forms of life could have been simple membranes made of fatty acids–also structures known to form spontaneously–that enveloped water and these self-replicating genetic molecules. The genetic material would encode the traits that each generation handed down to the next, just as DNA does in all things that are alive today. Fortuitous mutations, appearing at random in the copying process, would then propel evolution, enabling these early cells to adapt to their environment, to compete with one another, and eventually to turn into the life-forms we know.

The actual nature of the first organisms and the exact circumstances of the origin of life may be forever lost to science. But research can at least help us understand what is possible. The ultimate challenge is to construct an artificial organism that can reproduce and evolve. Creating life anew will certainly help us understand how life can start, how likely it is that it exists on other worlds and, ultimately, what life is.

Got to Start Somewhere

One of the most difficult and interesting mysteries surrounding the origin of life is exactly how the genetic material could have formed starting from simpler molecules present on the early earth. Judging from the roles that RNA has in modern cells, it seems likely that RNA appeared before DNA. When modern cells make proteins, they first copy genes from DNA into RNA and then use the RNA as a blueprint to make proteins. This last stage could have existed independently at first. Later on, DNA could have appeared as a more permanent form of storage, thanks to its superior chemical stability.

Investigators have one more reason for thinking that RNA came before DNA. The RNA versions of enzymes, called ribozymes, also serve a pivotal role in modern cells. The structures that translate RNA into proteins are hybrid RNA-protein machines, and it is the RNA in them that does the catalytic work. Thus, each of our cells appears to carry in its ribosomes "fossil" evidence of a primordial RNA world.

Much research, therefore, has focused on understanding the possible origin of RNA. Genetic molecules such as DNA and

RNA are polymers (strings of smaller molecules) made of building blocks called nucleotides. In turn, nucleotides have three distinct components: a sugar, a phosphate, and a nucleobase. Nucleobases come in four types and constitute the alphabet in which the polymer encodes information. In a DNA nucleotide the nucleobase can be A, G, C, or T, standing for the molecules adenine, guanine, cytosine, or thymine; in the RNA alphabet the letter U, for uracil, replaces the T. The nucleobases are nitrogen-rich compounds that bind to one another according to a simple rule; thus, A pairs with U (or T), and G pairs with C. Such base pairs form the rungs of DNA's twisted ladder–the familiar double helix–and their exclusive pairings are crucial for faithfully copying the information so a cell can reproduce. Meanwhile the phosphate and sugar molecules form the backbone of each strand of DNA or RNA.

Nucleobases can assemble spontaneously, in a series of steps, from cyanide, acetylene, and water–simple molecules that were certainly present in the primordial mix of chemicals. Sugars are also easy to assemble from simple starting materials. It has been known for well over 100 years that mixtures of many types of sugar molecules can be obtained by warming an alkaline solution of formaldehyde, which also would have been available on the young planet. The problem, however, is how to obtain the "right" kind of sugar–ribose, in the case of RNA–to make nucleotides. Ribose, along with three closely related sugars, can form from the reaction of two simpler sugars that contain two and three carbon atoms, respectively. Ribose's ability to form in that way does not solve the problem of how it became abundant on the early earth, however, because it turns out that ribose is unstable and rapidly breaks down in an even mildly alkaline solution. In the past, this observation has led many researchers to conclude that the first genetic molecules could not have contained ribose. But one of us (Ricardo) and others have discovered ways in which ribose could have been stabilized.

The phosphate part of nucleotides presents another intriguing puzzle. Phosphorus–the central element of the phosphate group–is abundant in the earth's crust but mostly in minerals that do not dissolve readily in water, where life presumably originated. So it is not obvious how phosphates would have gotten into the prebiotic mix. The high temperatures of volcanic vents can convert phosphate-containing minerals to soluble forms of phosphate, but the amounts released, at least near modern volcanoes, are small. A completely different potential source of phosphorus compounds is schreibersite, a mineral commonly found in certain meteors.

In 2005 Matthew Pasek and Dante Lauretta of the University of Arizona discovered that the corrosion of schreibersite in water releases its phosphorus component. This pathway seems promising because it releases phosphorus in a form that is both much more soluble in water than phosphate and much more reactive with organic (carbon-based) compounds.

Some Assembly Required

Given that we have at least an outline of potential pathways leading to the nucleobases, sugars, and phosphate, the next logical step would be to properly connect these components. This step, however, is the one that has caused the most intense frustration in prebiotic chemistry research for the past several decades. Simply mixing the three components in water does not lead to the spontaneous formation of a nucleotide–largely because each joining reaction also involves the release of a water molecule, which does not often occur spontaneously in a watery solution. For the needed chemical bonds to form, energy must be supplied, for example, by adding energy-rich compounds that aid in the reaction. Many such compounds may have existed on the early earth. In the laboratory, however, reactions powered by such molecules have proved to be inefficient at best and in most cases completely unsuccessful.

This spring–to the field's great excitement–John Sutherland and his co-workers at the University of Manchester in England announced that they found a much more plausible way that nucleotides could have formed, which also sidesteps the issue of ribose's instability. These creative chemists abandoned the tradition of attempting to make nucleotides by joining a nucleobase, sugar, and phosphate. Their approach relies on the same simple starting materials employed previously, such as derivatives of cyanide, acetylene, and formaldehyde. But instead of forming nucleobase and ribose separately and then trying to join them, the team mixed the starting ingredients together, along with phosphate. A complex web of reactions–with phosphate acting as a crucial catalyst at several steps along the way–produced a small molecule called 2-aminooxazole, which can be viewed as a fragment of a sugar joined to a piece of a nucleobase.

A crucial feature of this small, stable molecule is that it is very volatile. Perhaps small amounts of 2-aminooxazole formed together with a mixture of other chemicals in a pond on the early earth; once the water evaporated, the 2-aminooxazole vaporized, only to condense elsewhere, in a purified form. There it would accumulate as a reservoir of material, ready for further chemical reactions that would form a full sugar and nucleobase attached to each other.

Another important and satisfying aspect of this chain of reactions is that some of the early-stage by-products facilitate transformations at later stages in of the process. Elegant as it is, the pathway does not generate exclusively the "correct" nucleotides: in some cases, the sugar and nucleobase are not joined in the proper spatial arrangement. But amazingly, exposure to ultraviolet light–intense solar UV rays hit shallow waters on the early earth–destroys the "incorrect" nucleotides and leaves behind the "correct" ones. The end result is a remarkably clean route to the C and U nucleotides. Of course, we still need a route to G and A, so challenges remain. But the work by Sutherland's team is a major step toward explaining how a molecule as complex as RNA could have formed on the early earth.

Some Warm, Little Vial

Once we have nucleotides, the final step in the formation of an RNA molecule is polymerization: the sugar of one nucleotide forms a chemical bond with the phosphate of the next, so that nucleotides string themselves together into a chain. Once again, in water the bonds do not form spontaneously and instead require some external energy. By adding various chemicals to a solution of chemically reactive versions of the nucleotides, researchers have been able to produce short chains of RNA, two to 40 nucleotides long. In the late 1990s Jim Ferris and his coworkers at the Rensselaer Polytechnic Institute showed that clay minerals enhance the process, producing chains of up to 50 or so nucleotides. (A typical gene today is thousands to millions of nucleotides long.) The minerals' intrinsic ability to bind nucleotides brings reactive molecules close together, thereby facilitating the formation of bonds between them.

The discovery reinforced the suggestion by some researchers that life may have started on mineral surfaces, perhaps in clay-rich muds at the bottom of pools of water formed by hot springs [see "Life's Rocky Start," by Robert M. Hazen; *Scientific American*, April 2001].

Certainly finding out how genetic polymers first arose would not by itself solve the problem of the origin of life. To be "alive," organisms must be able to go forth and multiply–a process that includes copying genetic information. In modern cells enzymes, which are protein-based, carry out this copying function.

But genetic polymers, if they are made of the right sequences of nucleotides, can fold into complex shapes and can catalyze chemical reactions, just as today's enzymes do. Hence, it seems plausible that RNA in the very first organisms could have directed its own replication. This notion has inspired several experiments, both at our lab and at David Bartel's lab at the Massachusetts Institute of Technology, in which we "evolved" new ribozymes.

We started with trillions of random RNA sequences. Then we selected the ones that had catalytic properties, and we made copies of those. At each round of copying some of the new RNA strands underwent mutations that turned them into more efficient catalysts, and once again we singled those out for the next round of copying. By this directed evolution we were able to produce ribozymes that can catalyze the copying of relatively short strands of other RNAs, although they fall far short of being able to copy polymers with their own sequences into progeny RNAs.

Recently the principle of RNA self-replication received a boost from Tracey Lincoln and Gerald Joyce of the Scripps Research Institute, who evolved two RNA ribozymes, each of which could make copies of the other by joining together two shorter RNA strands. Unfortunately, success in the experiments required the presence of preexisting RNA pieces that were far too long and complex to have accumulated spontaneously. Still, the results suggest that RNA has the raw catalytic power to catalyze its own replication.

Is there a simpler alternative? We and others are now exploring chemical ways of copying genetic molecules without the aid of catalysts. In recent experiments, we started with single, "template" strands of DNA. (We used DNA because it is cheaper and easier to work with, but we could just as well have used RNA.) We mixed the templates in a solution containing isolated nucleotides to see if nucleotides would bind to the template through complementary base pairing (A joining to T and C to G) and then polymerize, thus forming a full double strand. This would be the first step to full replication: once a double strand had formed, separation of the strands would allow the complement to serve as a template for copying the original strand. With standard DNA or RNA, the process is exceedingly slow. But small changes to the chemical structure of the sugar component–changing one oxygen-hydrogen pair to an amino group (made of nitrogen and hydrogen)–made the polymerization hundreds of times faster, so that complementary strands formed in hours instead of weeks. The new polymer behaved much like classic RNA despite having nitrogen-phosphorus bonds instead of the normal oxygen-phosphorus bonds.

Boundary Issues

If we assume for the moment that the gaps in our understanding of the chemistry of life's origin will someday be filled, we can begin to consider how molecules might have interacted to assemble into the first cell-like structures, or "protocells."

The membranes that envelop all modern cells consist primarily of a lipid bilayer: a double sheet of such oily molecules as phospholipids and cholesterol. Membranes keep a cell's components physically together and form a barrier to the uncontrolled passage of large molecules. Sophisticated proteins embedded in the membrane act as gatekeepers and pump molecules in and out of the cell, while other proteins assist in the construction and repair of the membrane. How on earth could a rudimentary protocell, lacking protein machinery, carry out these tasks?

Primitive membranes were probably made of simpler molecules, such as fatty acids (which are one component of the more complex phospholipids). Studies in the late 1970s showed that membranes could indeed assemble spontaneously from plain fatty acids, but the general feeling was that these membranes would still pose a formidable barrier to the entry of nucleotides and other complex nutrients into the cell. This notion suggested that cellular metabolism had to develop first, so that cells could synthesize nucleotides for themselves. Work in our lab has shown, however, that molecules as large as nucleotides can in fact easily slip across membranes as long as both nucleotides and membranes are simpler, more "primitive" versions of their modern counterparts.

This finding allowed us to carry out a simple experiment modeling the ability of a protocell to copy its genetic information using environmentally supplied nutrients. We prepared fatty acid–based membrane vesicles containing a short piece of single-stranded DNA. As before, the DNA was meant to serve as a template for a new strand. Next, we exposed these vesicles to chemically reactive versions of nucleotides. The nucleotides crossed the membrane spontaneously and, once inside the model protocell, lined up on the DNA strand and reacted with one another to generate a complementary strand. The experiment supports the idea that the first protocells contained RNA (or something similar to it) and little else and replicated their genetic material without enzymes.

Let There Be Division

For protocells to start reproducing, they would have had to be able to grow, duplicate their genetic contents and divide into equivalent "daughter" cells. Experiments have shown that primitive vesicles can grow in at least two distinct ways. In pioneering work in the 1990s, Pier Luigi Luisi and his colleagues at the Swiss Federal Institute of Technology in Zurich added fresh fatty acids to the water surrounding such vesicles. In response, the membranes incorporated the fatty acids and grew in surface area. As water and dissolved substances slowly entered the interior, the cell's volume also increased.

A second approach, which was explored in our lab by then-graduate student Irene Chen, involved competition between protocells. Model protocells filled with RNA or similar materials became swollen, an osmotic effect resulting from the attempt of water to enter the cell and equalize its concentration inside and outside. The membrane of such swollen vesicles thus came under tension, and this tension drove growth, because adding new molecules relaxes the tension on the membrane, lowering the energy of the system. In fact, swollen vesicles grew by stealing fatty acids from relaxed neighboring vesicles, which shrank.

In the past year Ting Zhu, a graduate student in our lab, has observed the growth of model protocells after feeding them fresh fatty acids. To our amazement, the initially spherical vesicles did not grow simply by getting larger. Instead they first extended a thin filament. Over about half an hour, this protruding filament grew longer and thicker, gradually transforming the entire initial vesicle into a long, thin tube. This structure was quite delicate, and gentle shaking (such as might occur as wind generates waves on a pond) caused it to break into a number of smaller, spherical daughter protocells, which then grew larger and repeated the cycle.

Given the right building blocks, then, the formation of protocells does not seem that difficult: membranes self-assemble, genetic polymers self-assemble, and the two components can be brought together in a variety of ways, for example, if the membranes form around preexisting polymers. These sacs of water and RNA will also grow, absorb new molecules, compete for nutrients, and divide. But to become alive, they would also need to reproduce and evolve. In particular, they need to separate their RNA double strands so each single strand can act as a template for a new double strand that can be handed down to a daughter cell.

This process would not have started on its own, but it could have with a little help. Imagine, for example, a volcanic region on the otherwise cold surface of the early earth (at the time, the sun shone at only 70 percent of its current power). There could be pools of cold water, perhaps partly covered by ice but kept liquid by hot rocks. The temperature differences would cause convection currents, so that every now and then protocells in the water would be exposed to a burst of heat as they passed near the hot rocks, but they would almost instantly cool down again as the heated water mixed with the bulk of the cold water. The sudden heating would cause a double helix to separate into single strands. Once back in the cool region, new double strands—copies of the original one—could form as the single strands acted as templates.

As soon as the environment nudged protocells to start reproducing, evolution kicked in. In particular, at some point some of the RNA sequences mutated, becoming ribozymes that sped up the copying of RNA—thus adding a competitive advantage. Eventually ribozymes began to copy RNA without external help.

It is relatively easy to imagine how RNA-based protocells may have then evolved. Metabolism could have arisen gradually, as new ribozymes enabled cells to synthesize nutrients internally from simpler and more abundant starting materials. Next, the organisms might have added protein making to their bag of chemical tricks.

With their astonishing versatility, proteins would have then taken over RNA's role in assisting genetic copying and metabolism. Later, the organisms would have "learned" to make DNA, gaining the advantage of possessing a more robust carrier of genetic information.

At that point, the RNA world became the DNA world, and life as we know it began.

About the Authors

Alonso Ricardo, who was born in Cali, Colombia, is a research associate at the Howard Hughes Medical Institute at Harvard University. He has a long-standing interest in the origin of life and is now studying self-replicating chemical systems.

Jack W. Szostak is professor of genetics at Harvard Medical School and Massachusetts General Hospital. His interest in the laboratory construction of biological structures as a means of testing our understanding of how biology works dates back to the artificial chromosomes he described in the November 1987 Scientific American.

Looking for Life in the Multiverse

By Alejandro Jenkins, Gilad Perez

The typical Hollywood action hero skirts death for a living. Time and again, scores of bad guys shoot at him from multiple directions but miss by a hair. Cars explode just a fraction of a second too late for the fireball to catch him before he finds cover. And friends come to the rescue just before a villain's knife slits his throat. If any one of those things happened just a little differently, the hero would be hasta la vista, baby. Yet even if we have not seen the movie before, something tells us that he will make it to the end in one piece.

In some respects, the story of our universe resembles a Hollywood action movie. Several physicists have argued that a slight change to one of the laws of physics would cause some disaster that would disrupt the normal evolution of the universe and make our existence impossible. For example, if the strong nuclear force that binds together atomic nuclei had been slightly stronger or weaker, stars would have forged very little of the carbon and other elements that seem necessary to form planets, let alone life. If the proton were just 0.2 percent heavier than it is, all primordial hydrogen would have decayed almost immediately into neutrons, and no atoms would have formed. The list goes on.

The laws of physics—and in particular the constants of nature that enter into those laws, such as the strengths of the fundamental forces—might therefore seem finely tuned to make our existence possible. Short of invoking a supernatural explanation, which would be by definition outside the scope of science, a number of physicists and cosmologists began in the 1970s to try solving the puzzle by hypothesizing that our universe is just one of many existing universes, each with its own laws. According to this "anthropic" reasoning, we might just occupy the rare universe where the right conditions happen to have come together to make life possible.

Amazingly, the prevailing theory in modern cosmology, which emerged in the 1980s, suggests that such "parallel universes" may really exist–in fact, that a multitude of universes would incessantly pop out of a primordial vacuum the way ours did in the big bang. Our universe would be but one of many pocket universes within a wider expanse called the multiverse. In the overwhelming majority of those universes, the laws of physics might not allow the formation of matter as we know it or of galaxies, stars, planets, and life. But given the sheer number of possibilities, nature would have had a good chance to get the "right" set of laws at least once.

Our recent studies, however, suggest that some of these other universes–assuming they exist–may not be so inhospitable after all. Remarkably, we have found examples of alternative values of the fundamental constants, and thus of alternative sets of physical laws, that might still lead to very interesting worlds and perhaps to life. The basic idea is to change one aspect of the laws of nature and then make compensatory changes to other aspects.

Our work did not address the most serious fine-tuning problem in theoretical physics: the smallness of the "cosmological constant," thanks to which our universe neither recollapsed into nothingness a fraction of a second after the big bang, nor was ripped part by an exponentially accelerating expansion. Nevertheless, the examples of alternative, potentially habitable universes raise interesting questions and motivate further research into how unique our own universe might be.

The Weakless Way of Life

The conventional way scientists find out if one particular constant of nature is finely tuned or not is to turn that "constant" into an adjustable parameter and tweak it while leaving all other constants unaltered. Based on their newly modified laws of physics, the scientists then "play the movie" of the universe–they do calculations, what-if scenarios or computer simulations–to see what disaster occurs first. But there is no reason why one should tweak only one parameter at a time. That situation resembles trying to drive a car by varying only your latitude or only your longitude, but not both: unless you are traveling on a grid, you are destined to run off the road. Instead one can tweak multiple parameters at once.

To search for alternative sets of laws that still give rise to complex structures capable of sustaining life, one of us (Perez) and his collaborators did not make just small tweaks to the known laws of physics: they completely eliminated one of the four known fundamental forces of nature.

By their very name, the fundamental forces sound like indispensable features of any self-respecting universe. Without the strong nuclear force to bind quarks into protons and neutrons and those into atomic nuclei, matter as we know it would not exist. Without the electromagnetic force, there would be no light; there would also be no atoms and no chemical bonds. Without gravity, there would be no force to coalesce matter into galaxies, stars, and planets.

The fourth force, the weak nuclear force, has a subtler presence in our everyday life but still has played a major role in the history of our universe. Among other things, the weak force enables the reactions that turn neutrons into protons, and vice versa. In the first instants of the big bang, after quarks (among the first forms of matter to appear) had united in groups of three to form protons and neutrons, collectively called baryons, groups of four protons were then able to fuse together and become helium 4 nuclei, made of two protons and two neutrons. This so-called big bang nucleosynthesis took place a few seconds into the life of our universe, when it was already cold enough for baryons to form but still hot enough for the baryons to undergo nuclear fusion. Big bang nucleosynthesis produced the hydrogen and helium that would later form stars, where nuclear fusion and other processes would forge virtually all other naturally occurring elements. And to this day, the fusion of four protons to make helium 4 continues inside our sun, where it produces most of the energy that we receive from it.

Without the weak nuclear force, then, it seems unlikely that a universe could contain anything resembling complex chemistry, let alone life. Yet in 2006 Perez's team discovered a set of physical laws that relied on only the other three forces of nature and still led to a congenial universe.

Eliminating the weak nuclear force required several modifications to the so-called Standard Model of particle physics, the theory that describes all forces except gravity. The team showed that the tweaks could be done in such a way that the behavior of the other three forces–and other crucial parameters such as the masses of the quarks–would be the same as in our world. We should stress that this choice was a conservative one, intended to facilitate the calculation of how the universe would unfold. It is quite possible that a wide range of other "weakless" universes exist that are habitable but look nothing like our own.

In the weakless universe, the usual fusing of protons to form helium would be impossible, because it requires that two of the protons convert into neutrons. But other pathways could exist for the creation of the elements. For example, our universe contains overwhelmingly more matter than antimatter, but a small adjustment to the parameter that controls this asymmetry is enough to ensure that the big bang nucleosynthesis would leave behind a substantial amount of deuterium nuclei. Deuterium, also known as hydrogen 2, is the isotope of hydrogen whose nucleus contains a neutron in addition to the usual proton. Stars could then shine by fusing a proton and a deuterium nucleus to make a helium 3 (two protons and one neutron) nucleus.

Such weakless stars would be colder and smaller than the stars in our own universe. According to computer simulations by astrophysicist Adam Burrows of Princeton University, they could burn for about 7 billion years–about the current age of our sun–and radiate energy at a rate that would be a few percent of that of the sun.

Next Generation

Just like stars in our universe, weakless stars could synthesize elements as heavy as iron through further nuclear fusion. But the typical reactions that in our stars lead to elements beyond iron would be compromised, primarily because few neutrons would be available for nuclei to capture to become heavier isotopes, the first step in the formation of heavier elements. Small amounts of heavy elements, up to strontium, might still be synthesized inside weakless stars by other mechanisms.

In our universe, supernova explosions disperse the newly synthesized elements into space, and synthesize more of the elements themselves. Supernovae can be of several types: in the weakless universe, the supernova explosions caused by collapsing ultramassive stars would fail, because it is the emission of neutrinos, produced via the weak-force interactions, that transmits energy out of a star's core so as to sustain the shock wave that is causing the explosion. But a different type of supernova–the thermonuclear explosion of a star triggered by accretion, rather than by gravitational collapse–would still take place. Thus, elements could be dispersed into interstellar space, where they could seed new stars and planets.

Given the relative coldness of the weakless stars, a weakless Earth-like body would have to be about six times closer to its sun to stay as warm as our own Earth. To the inhabitants of such a planet, the sun would look much bigger. Weakless Earths would be significantly different from our own Earth in other ways. In our world, plate tectonics and volcanic activity are powered by the radioactive decay of uranium and thorium deep within Earth. Without these heavy elements, a typical weakless Earth might have a comparatively boring and featureless geology–except if gravitational processes provided an alternative source of heating, as happens on some moons of Saturn and Jupiter.

Chemistry, on the other hand, would be very similar to that of our world. One difference would be that the periodic table would stop at iron, except for extremely small traces of other elements. But this limitation should not prevent life-forms similar to the ones we know from evolving. Thus, even a universe with just three fundamental forces could be congenial to life.

Another approach, pursued by the other of us (Jenkins) and his collaborators, searches for alternative sets of laws by making smaller tweaks to the Standard Model than in the case of the weakless universe, though still involving multiple parameters at once. In 2008 the group studied to what extent the masses of the three lightest of the six quarks—called the up, down, and strange quarks—may vary without making organic chemistry impossible. Changing the quark masses will inevitably affect which baryons and which atomic nuclei can exist without decaying quickly. In turn, the different assortment of atomic nuclei will affect chemistry.

Quarky Chemistry

It seems plausible that intelligent life (if it is not very different from us) requires some form of organic chemistry, which is by definition the chemistry that involves carbon. The chemical properties of carbon follow from the fact that its nucleus has an electric charge of 6, so that six electrons orbit in a neutral carbon atom. These properties allow carbon to form an immense variety of complex molecules. (The suggestion often made by science-fiction writers that life could instead be based on silicon—the next element in carbon's group in the periodic table—is questionable: no silicon-based molecules of any significant degree of complexity are known to exist.) Furthermore, for complex organic molecules to form, elements with the chemistry of hydrogen (charge 1) and oxygen (charge 8) need to be present. To see if they could maintain organic chemistry, then, the team had to calculate whether nuclei of charge 1, 6, or 8 would decay radioactively before they could participate in chemical reactions.

The stability of a nucleus partly depends on its mass, which in turn depends on the masses of the baryons it is made of. Computing the masses of baryons and nuclei starting from the masses of the quarks is extremely challenging even in our universe. But after tweaking the intensity of the interaction between quarks, one can use the baryon masses measured in our universe to estimate how small changes to the masses of the quarks would affect the masses of nuclei.

In our world, the neutron is roughly 0.1 percent heavier than the proton. If the masses of the quarks were changed so that the neutron became 2 percent heavier than the proton, no long-lived form of carbon or oxygen would exist. If quark masses were adjusted to make the proton heavier than the neutron, then the proton in a hydrogen nucleus would capture the surrounding electron and turn into a neutron, so that hydrogen atoms could not exist for very long. But deuterium or tritium (hydrogen 3) might still be stable, and so would some forms of oxygen and carbon. Indeed, we found that only if the proton became heavier than the neutron by more than about 1 percent would there cease to be some stable form of hydrogen.

With deuterium (or tritium) substituting for hydrogen 1, oceans would be made of heavy water, which has subtly different physical and chemical properties from ordinary water. Still, there does not appear to be a fundamental obstacle in these worlds to some form of organic life evolving.

In our world, the third-lightest quark–the strange quark–is too heavy to participate in nuclear physics. But if its mass were reduced by a factor of more than about 10, nuclei could be made not just of protons and neutrons but also of other baryons containing strange quarks.

For example, the team identified a universe in which the up and strange quark would have roughly the same mass, whereas the down quark would be much lighter. Then atomic nuclei would not be made of protons and neutrons but instead of neutrons and another baryon, called the $\Sigma-$ ("sigma minus"). Remarkably, even such a radically different universe would have stable forms of hydrogen, carbon and oxygen and therefore could have organic chemistry.

Whether those elements would be produced abundantly enough for life to evolve somewhere within them is an unanswered question.

But if life can arise, it would again happen much like it does in our world. Physicists in such a universe might be puzzled by the fact that the up and strange quarks would have almost identical masses. They might even imagine that this amazing coincidence has an anthropic explanation, based on the need for organic chemistry. We know, however, that such an explanation would be wrong, because our world has organic chemistry even though the masses of the down and strange quarks are quite different.

On the other hand, universes in which the three light quarks had roughly the same masses would probably have no organic chemistry: any nucleus with more than a couple of units of electrical charge would decay away almost immediately. Unfortunately, it is very difficult to map out in detail the histories of universes whose physical parameters are different from our own. This issue requires further research.

String Landscaping

Fine-tuning has been invoked by some theoretical physicists as indirect evidence for the multiverse. Do our findings therefore call the concept of a multiverse into question? We do not think that this is necessarily the case, for two reasons. The first comes from observation, combined with theory. Astronomical data strongly support the hypothesis that our universe started out as a tiny patch of spacetime, perhaps as small as a billionth the size of a proton, which then went through a phase of rapid, exponential growth, called inflation. Cosmology still lacks a definitive theoretical model for inflation, but theory suggests that different patches could inflate at different rates and that each patch could form a "pocket" that can become a universe in its own right, characterized by its own values for the constants of nature [see "The Self-Reproducing Inflationary Universe," by Andrei Linde; *Scientific American*, November 1994]. Space between pocket universes would keep expanding so fast that it would be impossible to travel or send messages from one pocket to the next, even at the speed of light.

The second reason to suspect the existence of the multiverse is that one quantity still seems to be finely tuned to an extraordinary degree: the cosmological constant, which represents the amount of energy embodied in empty space. Quantum physics predicts that even otherwise empty space must contain energy. Einstein's general theory of relativity requires that all forms of energy exert gravity. If this energy is positive, it causes spacetime to expand at an exponentially accelerating rate. If it is negative, the universe would recollapse in a "big crunch." Quantum theory seems to imply that the cosmological constant should be so large–in the positive or negative direction–that space would expand too quickly for structures such as galaxies to have a chance to form or else that the universe would exist for a fraction of a second before recollapsing.

One way to explain why our universe avoided such disasters could be that some other term in the equations canceled out the effects of the cosmological constant. The trouble is that this term would have to be fine-tuned with exquisite precision. A deviation in even the 100th decimal place would lead to a universe without any significant structure.

In 1987 Steven Weinberg, the Nobel Prize–winning theorist at the University of Texas at Austin, proposed an anthropic explanation. He calculated an upper bound on the value of the cosmological constant that would still be compatible with life. Were the value any bigger, space would expand so quickly that the universe would lack the structures that life requires. In a way, then, our very existence predicts the low value of the constant.

Then, in the late 1990s, astronomers discovered that the universe is indeed expanding at an accelerating rate, pushed by a mysterious form of "dark energy." The observed rate implied that the cosmological constant is positive and tiny–within the bounds of Weinberg's prediction–meaning that dark energy is very dilute.

Thus, the cosmological constant seems to be fine-tuned to an exceptional degree. Moreover, the methods our teams have applied to the weak nuclear force and to the masses of quarks seem to fail in this case, because it seems impossible to find congenial universes in which the cosmological constant is substantially larger than the value we observe. Within a multiverse, the vast majority of universes could have cosmological constants incompatible with the formation of any structure.

A real-world analogy—as opposed to an action-movie one—would be to send thousands of people trekking across a mountainous desert. The few who make it out alive might tell stories full of cliffhangers, encounters with poisonous snakes, and other brushes with death that would seem too close to be realistic.

Theoretical arguments rooted in string theory—a speculative extension of the Standard Model that attempts to describe all forces as the vibrations of microscopic strings—seem to confirm such a scenario. These arguments suggest that during inflation the cosmological constant and other parameters could have taken a virtually limitless range of different values, called the string theory landscape [see "The String Theory Landscape," by Raphael Bousso and Joseph Polchinski; *Scientific American*, September 2004].

Our own work, however, does cast some doubt on the usefulness of anthropic reasoning, at least beyond the case of the cosmological constant. It also raises important questions. For example, if life really is possible in a weakless universe, then why does our own universe have a weak force at all? In fact, particle physicists consider the weak force in our universe to be, in a sense, not weak enough. Its observed value seems unnaturally strong within the Standard Model. (The leading explanation for this mystery requires the existence of new particles and forces that physicists hope to discover at the newly opened Large Hadron Collider at CERN near Geneva.)

As a consequence, many theorists expect that most universes would have weak interactions that are so feeble as to be effectively absent. The real challenge, then, may be to explain why we do not live in a weakless universe.

Eventually only a deeper knowledge of how universes are born can answer such questions. In particular, we may discover physical principles of a more fundamental level that imply that nature prefers certain sets of laws over others.

We may never find any direct evidence of the existence of other universes, and we certainly will never get to visit one. But we may need to learn more about them if we want to understand what is our true place in the multiverse–or whatever it is that is out there.

About the Authors

Alejandro Jenkins, a native of Costa Rica, is in the High Energy Physics group at Florida State University. He has degrees from Harvard University and the California Institute of Technology, and he investigated alternative universes while at the Massachusetts Institute of Technology with Bob Jaffe and Itamar Kimchi.

Gilad Perez is a theorist at the Weizmann Institute of Science in Rehovot, Israel, where he received his Ph.D. in 2003. While at Lawrence Berkeley National Lab, he explored the multiverse with Roni Harnik of Stanford University and Graham D. Kribs of the University of Oregon. He has also done stints at Stony Brook University, Boston University and Harvard.

Our Improbable Existence Is No Evidence for a Multiverse

By Philip Goff

We exist, and we are living creatures. It follows that the universe we live in must be compatible with the existence of life. However, as scientists have studied the fundamental principles that govern our universe, they have discovered that the odds of a universe like ours being compatible with life are astronomically low. We can model what the universe would have looked like if its constants—the strength of gravity, the mass of an electron, the cosmological constant—had been slightly different. What has become clear is that, across a huge range of these constants, they had to have pretty much exactly the values they had in order for life to be possible. The physicist Lee Smolin has calculated that the odds of life-compatible numbers coming up by chance is 1 in 10,229.

Physicists refer to this discovery as the "fine-tuning" of physics for life. What should we make of it? Some take this to be evidence of nothing other than our good fortune. But many prominent scientists—Martin Rees, Alan Guth, Max Tegmark—have taken it to be evidence that we live in a multiverse: that our universe is just one of a huge, perhaps infinite, ensemble of worlds. The hope is that this allows us to give a "monkeys on typewriters" explanation of the fine-tuning. If you have enough monkeys randomly jabbing away on typewriters, it becomes not so improbable that one will happen to write a bit of English. By analogy, if there are enough universes, with enough variation in the numbers in their physics, then it becomes statistically likely that one will happen to have the right numbers for life.

This explanation makes intuitive sense. However, experts in the mathematics of probability have identified the inference from the fine-tuning to the multiverse as an instance of fallacious reasoning. Specifically, multiverse theorists commit the inverse gambler's fallacy, which is a slight twist on the regular gambler's fallacy. In the regular gambler's fallacy, the gambler has been at the casino all night and has had a terrible run of bad luck. She thinks to herself, "My next roll of the dice is bound to be a good one, as it's unlikely I'd roll badly all night!" This is a fallacy, because for any particular roll, the odds of, say, getting a double six are the same: 1/36. How many times the gambler has rolled that night has no bearing on whether the next roll will be a double six.

In the inverse gambler's fallacy, a visitor walks into a casino and the first thing she sees is someone rolling a double six. She thinks "Wow, that person must've been playing for a long time, as it's unlikely they'd have such good luck just from one roll." This is fallacious for the same reason. The casino- visitor has only observed one roll of the dice, and the odds of that one roll coming good is the same as any other roll: 1/36. How long the player has been rolling prior to this moment has no bearing on the odds of the one roll the visitor observed being a double six.

Philosopher Ian Hacking was the first to connect the inverse gambler's fallacy to arguments for the multiverse, focusing on physicist John Wheeler's oscillating universe theory, which held that our universe is the latest of a long temporal sequence of universes. Just as the casino-visitor says "Wow, that person must've been playing for a long time, as it's unlikely they'd have such good luck just from one roll," so the multiverse theorist says "Wow, there must be many other universes before this one, as it's unlikely the right numbers would have come up if there'd only been one."

Other theorists later realized that the charge applies quite generally to every attempt to derive a multiverse from fine-tuning. Consider the following analogy. You wake up with amnesia, with no clue as to how you got where you are. In front of you is a monkey bashing away on a typewriter, writing perfect English. This clearly requires explanation. You might think: "Maybe I'm dreaming ... maybe this is a trained monkey ... maybe it's a robot." What you would not think is "There must be lots of other monkeys around here, mostly writing nonsense." You wouldn't think this because what needs explaining is why this monkey–the only one you've actually observed–is writing English, and postulating other monkeys doesn't explain what this monkey is doing.

Some have objected that this argument against the inference from fine-tuning to a multiverse ignores the selection effect that exist in cases of fine-tuning, namely that fact that we could not possibly have observed a universe that wasn't fine-tuned. If the universe wasn't fine-tuned, then life would be impossible, and so nobody would be around to observe anything. It is of course true that this selection effect exists, but it makes no difference to whether or not the fallacy is committed. We can see this by just adding an artificial selection effect to the monkey and typewriter analogy of the last paragraph. Consider the following story:

You wake up to find yourself in a room sat opposite the Joker (from Batman) and a monkey called Joey on a typewriter. The Joker tells you that while you were unconscious, he decided to play a little game. He gave Joey one hour to bash on the typewriter, committing to release you if Joey wrote some English or to kill you before you regained consciousness if he didn't. Fortunately, Joey has typed "I love how yellow bananas are," and hence you are to be released.

In the above story, you could not possibly have observed Joey typing anything other than English–the Joker would have killed you before you had a chance–just as we could never have observed a non-fine-tuned universe. And yet the inference to many monkeys is still unwarranted. Given how unlikely it is that an ordinary monkey would come up with "I love how yellow bananas are" just by randomly bashing away, you might suspect some kind of trick. What you would not conclude, however, is that there must be many other monkeys typing rubbish. Again, what you need explaining is why Joey is typing English, and the postulation of other monkeys doesn't explain this. By analogy, what we need explaining is why the only universe we've ever observed is fine-tuned, and the postulation of other universes doesn't account for this.

But isn't there scientific evidence for a multiverse? Some physicists do indeed think there is a tentative empirical evidence for a kind of multiverse, that described by the hypothesis of eternal inflation. According to eternal inflation, there is a vast, exponentially expanding mega space in which certain regions slow down to form "bubble universes," our universe being one such bubble universe. However, there is no empirical ground for thinking that the constants of physics–the strength of gravity, the mass of electrons, etc.–are different in these different bubble universes. And without such variation, the fine-tuning problem is even worse: we now have a huge number of monkeys all of whom are typing English.

At this point, many bring in string theory. String theory offers a way to make sense of the possibility that the different bubbles might have different constants. On string theory, the supposedly "fixed" numbers of physics are determined by the phase of space, and there are 10500 different possible phases of space in the so-called "string landscape." It could be that random processes ensure that a wide variety of possibilities from the string landscape are realized in the different bubble universes. Again, however, there is no empirical reason for thinking that this possibility is actual.

The reason some scientists take seriously the possibility of a multiverse in which the constants vary in different universes is that it seems to explain the fine-tuning. But on closer examination, the inference from fine-tuning to the multiverse proves to be instance of flawed reasoning. So, what should we make of the fine-tuning? Perhaps there is some other way of explaining it. Or perhaps we just got lucky.

About the Author

Philip Goff is a philosopher and consciousness researcher at Durham University in the UK, and author of Galileo's Error: Foundations for a New Science of Consciousness. His research focuses on how to integrate consciousness into our scientific worldview.

Are Aliens Among Us?

By Paul Davies

The origin of life is one of the great unsolved problems of science. Nobody knows how, where, or when life originated. About all that is known for certain is that microbial life had established itself on Earth by about 3 1/2 billion years ago. In the absence of hard evidence of what came before, there is plenty of scope for disagreement.

Thirty years ago the prevailing view among biologists was that life resulted from a chemical fluke so improbable it would be unlikely to have happened twice in the observable universe. That conservative position was exemplified by Nobel Prize–winning French biologist Jacques Monod, who wrote in 1970: "Man at last knows that he is alone in the unfeeling immensity of the universe, out of which he emerged only by chance." In recent years, however, the mood has shifted dramatically. In 1995 renowned Belgian biochemist Christian de Duve called life "a cosmic imperative" and declared "it is almost bound to arise" on any Earth-like planet. De Duve's statement reinforced the belief among astrobiologists that the universe is teeming with life. Dubbed biological determinism by Robert Shapiro of New York University, this theory is sometimes expressed by saying that "life is written into the laws of nature."

How can scientists determine which view is correct? The most direct way is to seek evidence for life on another planet, such as Mars. If life originated from scratch on two planets in a single solar system, it would decisively confirm the hypothesis of biological determinism. Unfortunately, it may be a long time before missions to the Red Planet are sophisticated enough to hunt for Martian life-forms and, if they indeed exist, to study such extraterrestrial biota in detail.

An easier test of biological determinism may be possible, however. No planet is more Earth-like than Earth itself, so if life does emerge readily under terrestrial conditions, then perhaps it formed many times on our home planet. To pursue this tantalizing possibility, scientists have begun searching deserts, lakes, and caverns for evidence of "alien" life-forms–organisms that would differ fundamentally from all known living creatures because they arose independently. Most likely, such organisms would be microscopic, so researchers are devising tests to identify exotic microbes that could be living among us.

Scientists have yet to reach a consensus on a strict definition of life, but most would agree that two of its hallmarks are an ability to metabolize (to draw nutrients from the environment, convert those nutrients into energy, and excrete waste products) and an ability to reproduce. The orthodox view of biogenesis holds that if life on Earth originated more than once, one form would have swiftly predominated and eliminated all the others. This extermination might have happened, for example, if one form quickly appropriated all the available resources or "ganged up" on a weaker form of life by swapping successful genes exclusively with its own kind. But this argument is weak. Bacteria and archaea, two very different types of microorganisms that descended from a common ancestor more than three billion years ago, have peacefully coexisted ever since, without one eliminating the other. Moreover, alternative forms of life might not have directly competed with known organisms, either because the aliens occupied extreme environments where familiar microbes could not survive or because the two forms of life required different resources.

The Argument for Aliens

Even if alternative life does not exist now, it might have flourished in the distant past before dying out for some reason. In that case, scientists might still be able to find markers of their extinct biology in the geologic record. If alternative life had a distinctively different metabolism, say, it might have altered rocks or created mineral deposits in a way that cannot be explained by the activities of known organisms. Biomarkers in the form of distinctive organic molecules that could not have been created by familiar life might even be hiding in ancient microfossils, such as those found in rocks dating from the Archean era (more than 2.5 billion years ago).

A more exciting but also more speculative possibility is that alternative life-forms have survived and are still present in the environment, constituting a kind of shadow biosphere, a term coined by Carol Cleland and Shelley Copley of the University of Colorado at Boulder. At first this idea might seem preposterous; if alien organisms thrived right under our noses (or even in our noses), would not scientists have discovered them already? It turns out that the answer is no. The vast majority of organisms are microbes, and it is almost impossible to tell what they are simply by looking at them through a microscope. Microbiologists must analyze the genetic sequences of an organism to determine its location on the tree of life—the phylogenetic grouping of all known creatures—and researchers have classified only a tiny fraction of all observed microbes.

To be sure, all the organisms that have so far been studied in detail almost certainly descended from a common origin. Known organisms share a similar biochemistry and use an almost identical genetic code, which is why biologists can sequence their genes and position them on a single tree. But the procedures that researchers use to analyze newly discovered organisms are deliberately customized to detect life as we know it. These techniques would fail to respond correctly to a different biochemistry. If shadow life is confined to the microbial realm, it is entirely possible that scientists have overlooked it.

Ecologically Isolated Aliens

Where might investigators look for alien organisms on Earth today? Some scientists have focused on searching for organisms occupying a niche that is ecologically isolated, lying beyond the reach of ordinary known life. One of the surprising discoveries in recent years is the ability of known life to endure extraordinarily harsh conditions. Microbes have been found inhabiting extreme environments ranging from scalding volcanic vents to the dry valleys of Antarctica. Other so-called extremophiles can survive in salt-saturated lakes, highly acidic mine tailings contaminated with metals, and the waste pools of nuclear reactors.

Nevertheless, even the hardiest microorganisms have their limits. Life as we know it depends crucially on the availability of liquid water. In the Atacama Desert in northern Chile is a region that is so dry that all traces of familiar life are absent. Furthermore, although certain microbes can thrive in temperatures above the normal boiling point of water, scientists have not yet found anything living above about 130 degrees Celsius (266 degrees Fahrenheit). It is conceivable, though, that an exotic alternative form of life could exist under more extreme conditions of dryness or temperature.

Thus, scientists might find evidence for alternative life by discovering signs of biological activity, such as the cycling of carbon between the ground and the atmosphere, in an ecologically isolated region. The obvious places to look for such disconnected ecosystems are in the deep subsurface of Earth's crust, in the upper atmosphere, in Antarctica, in salt mines, and in sites contaminated by metals and other pollutants. Alternatively, researchers could vary parameters such as temperature and moisture in a laboratory experiment until all known forms of life are extinguished; if some biological activity persists, it could be a sign of shadow life at work. Scientists used this technique to discover the radiation-resistant bacterium *Deinococcus radiodurans*, which can withstand gamma-ray doses that are 1,000 times as great as what would be lethal for humans. It turns out that *D. radiodurans* and all the other so-called radiophiles that researchers have identified are genetically linked to known life, so they are not candidate aliens, but that finding does not rule out the possibility of discovering alternative life-forms in this way.

Investigators have already pinpointed a handful of ecosystems that appear to be almost completely isolated from the rest of the biosphere. Located far underground, these microbial communities are cut off from light, oxygen, and the organic products of other organisms. They are sustained by the ability of some microbes to use carbon dioxide and hydrogen released by chemical reactions or radioactivity to metabolize, grow, and replicate. Although all the organisms found to date in these ecosystems are closely related to surface-dwelling microbes, the biological exploration of Earth's deep subsurface is still in its infancy, and many surprises may lie in store. The Integrated Ocean Drilling Program has been sampling rocks from the seabed to a depth approaching one kilometer, in part to explore their microbial content. Boreholes on land have revealed signs of biological activity from even deeper locations. So far, however, the research community has not conducted a systematic, large-scale program to probe the deep subsurface of Earth's crust for life.

Ecologically Integrated Aliens

One might suppose it would be easier to find alternative life-forms if they were not isolated but integrated into the known biosphere existing all around us. But if shadow life is restricted to alien microbes that are intermingled with familiar kinds, the exotic creatures would be very hard to spot on casual inspection. Microbial morphology is limited–most microorganisms are just little spheres or rods. Aliens might stand out biochemically, though. One way to search for them is to make a guess as to what alternative chemistry might be involved and then look for its distinctive signature.

A simple example involves chirality. Large biological molecules possess a definite handedness: although the atoms in a molecule can be configured into two mirror-image orientations–left-handed or right-handed–molecules must possess compatible chirality to assemble into more complex structures. In known life-forms, the amino acids—the building blocks of proteins—are left-handed, whereas the sugars are right-handed and DNA is a right-handed double helix. The laws of chemistry, however, are blind to left and right, so if life started again from scratch, there would be a 50–50 chance that its building blocks would be molecules of the opposite handedness. Shadow life could in principle be biochemically almost identical to known life but made of mirror-image molecules. Such mirror life would not compete directly with known life, nor could the two forms swap genes, because the relevant molecules would not be interchangeable.

Fortunately, researchers could identify mirror life using a very simple procedure. They could prepare a nutrient broth consisting entirely of the mirror images of the molecules usually included in a standard culture medium; a mirror organism might be able to consume the concoction with gusto, whereas a known life-form would find it unpalatable. Richard Hoover and Elena Pikuta of the NASA Marshall Space Flight Center recently performed a pilot experiment of this kind, putting a variety of newly discovered extremophiles into a mirror broth and then looking for biological activity. They found one microbe that grew in the broth, an organism dubbed *Anaerovirgula multivorans* that had been isolated from the sediments of an alkaline lake in California. Disappointingly, this organism did not turn out to be an example of mirror life; rather it was a bacterium with the surprising ability to chemically alter the amino acids and sugars of the wrong handedness so as to make them digestible. The study, however, looked at just a small fraction of the microbial realm.

Another possibility is that shadow life might share the same general biochemistry with familiar life but employ a different suite of amino acids or nucleotides (the building blocks of DNA). All known organisms use the same set of nucleotides—designated A, C, G, and T for their distinguishing bases (adenine, cytosine, guanine, and thymine)—to store information and, with rare exceptions, the same 20 amino acids to construct proteins, the workhorses of cells. The genetic code is based on triplets of nucleotides, with different triplets spelling out the names of different amino acids. The sequence of triplets in a gene dictates the sequence of amino acids that must be strung together to build a particular protein. But chemists can synthesize many other amino acids that are not present in known organisms. The Murchison meteorite, a cometary remnant that fell in Australia in 1969, contained many common amino acids but also some unusual ones, such as isovaline and pseudoleucine. (Scientists are not sure how the amino acids formed in the meteorite, but most researchers believe that the chemicals were not produced by biological activity.) Some of these unfamiliar amino acids might make suitable building blocks for alternative forms of life. To hunt for such aliens, investigators would need to identify an amino acid that is not used by any known organisms nor generated as a by-product of an organism's metabolism or decay, and to look for its presence in the environment, either among living microbes or in the organic detritus that might be generated by a shadow biosphere.

To help focus the search, scientists can glean clues from the burgeoning field of synthetic, or artificial, life. Biochemists are currently attempting to engineer completely novel organisms by inserting additional amino acids into proteins. A pioneer of this research, Steve Benner of the Foundation for Applied Molecular Evolution in Gainesville, Fla., has pointed out that a class of molecules known as alpha-methyl amino acids look promising for artificial life because they can fold properly. These molecules, however, have not been found in any natural organism studied to date. As investigators identify new microbes, it would be a relatively simple matter to use standard tools for analyzing the composition of proteins, such as mass spectrometry, to learn which amino acids the organisms contain. Any glaring oddities in the inventory would signal that the microbe could be a candidate for shadow life.

If such a strategy were successful, researchers would face the difficulty of determining whether they were dealing with a genuine alternative form of life descended from a separate origin or with merely a new domain of known life, such as archaea, which were not identified until the late 1970s. In other words, how can scientists be sure that what seems like a new tree of life is not in fact an undiscovered branch of the known tree that split away a very long time ago and has so far escaped our attention? In all likelihood, the earliest life-forms were radically different from those that followed. For example, the sophisticated triplet DNA code for specifying particular amino acids shows evidence of being optimized in its efficiency by evolutionary selection. This observation suggests the existence of a more rudimentary precursor, such as a doublet code employing only 10, rather than 20, amino acids. It is conceivable that some primitive organisms are still using the old precursor code today. Such microbes would not be truly alien but more like living fossils. Nevertheless, their discovery would still be of immense scientific interest. Another possible holdover from an earlier biological epoch would be microbes that use RNA in place of DNA.

The chance of confusing a separate tree of life with an undiscovered branch of our own tree is diminished if one considers more radical alternatives to known biochemistry. Astrobiologists have speculated about forms of life in which some other solvent (such as ethane or methane) replaces water, although it is hard to identify environments on Earth that would support any of the suggested substances. (Ethane and methane are liquid only in very cold places such as the surface of Titan, Saturn's largest moon.) Another popular conjecture concerns the basic chemical elements that make up the vital parts of known organisms: carbon, hydrogen, oxygen, nitrogen, and phosphorus. Would life be possible if a different element were substituted for one of these five?

Phosphorus is problematic for life in some ways. It is relatively rare and would not have existed in abundance in readily accessible, soluble form under the conditions that prevailed during the early history of Earth. Felisa Wolfe-Simon, formerly at Arizona State

University and now at Harvard University, has hypothesized that arsenic can successfully fill the role of phosphorus for living organisms and would have offered distinct chemical advantages in ancient environments. For example, in addition to doing all the things that phosphorus can do in the way of structural bonding and energy storage, arsenic could provide a source of energy to drive metabolism. (Arsenic is a poison for regular life precisely because it mimics phosphorus so well. Similarly, phosphorus would be poisonous to an arsenic-based organism.) Could it be that arseno-life still lingers in phosphorus-poor and arsenic-rich pockets, such as ocean vents and hot springs?

Another important variable is size. All known organisms manufacture proteins from amino acids using large molecular machines called ribosomes, which link the amino acids together. The need to accommodate ribosomes requires that all autonomous organisms on our tree of life must be at least a few hundred nanometers (billionths of a meter) across. Viruses are much smaller–as tiny as 20 nanometers wide–but these agents are not autonomous organisms because they cannot reproduce without the help of the cells they infect. Because of this dependence, viruses cannot be considered an alternative form of life, nor is there any evidence that they stem from an independent origin. But over the years several scientists have claimed that the biosphere is teeming with cells that are too small to accommodate ribosomes. In 1990 Robert Folk of the University of Texas at Austin drew attention to tiny spheroidal and ovoid objects in sedimentary rocks found in hot springs in Viterbo, Italy. Folk proposed that the objects were fossilized "nannobacteria" (a spelling he preferred), the calcified remains of organisms as small as 30 nanometers across. More recently, Philippa Uwins of the University of Queensland has discovered similar structures in rock samples from a deep-ocean borehole off the coast of Western Australia. If these structures indeed arise from biological processes–and many scientists hotly dispute this contention–they may be evidence of alternative life-forms that do not use ribosomes to assemble their proteins and that thus evade the lower size limit that applies to known life.

Perhaps the most intriguing possibility of all is that alien life-forms inhabit our own bodies. While observing mammalian cells with an electron microscope in 1988, Olavi Kajander and his colleagues at the University of Kuopio in Finland observed ultrasmall particles inside many of the cells. With dimensions as small as 50 nanometers, these particles were about one-10th the size of conventional small bacteria. Ten years later Kajander and his co-workers proposed that the particles were living organisms that thrive in urine and induce the formation of kidney stones by precipitating calcium and other minerals around themselves. Although such claims remain controversial, it is conceivable that at least some of these Lilliputian forms are alien organisms employing a radically alternative biochemistry.

What Is Life, Anyway?

If a biochemically weird microorganism should be discovered, its status as evidence for a second genesis, as opposed to a new branch on our own tree of life, will depend on how fundamentally it differs from known life. In the absence of an understanding of how life began, however, there are no hard-and-fast criteria for this distinction. For instance, some astrobiologists have speculated about the possibility of life arising from silicon compounds instead of carbon compounds. Because carbon is so central to our biochemistry, it is hard to imagine that silicon- and carbon-based organisms could have emerged from a common origin. On the other hand, an organism that employed the same suite of nucleotides and amino acids as known life-forms but merely used a different genetic code for specifying amino acids would not provide strong evidence for an independent origin, because the differences could probably be explained by evolutionary drift.

A converse problem also exists: dissimilar organisms subjected to similar environmental challenges will often gradually converge in their properties, which will become optimized for thriving under existing conditions. If this evolutionary convergence were strong enough, it could mask the evidence for independent biogenesis events. For example, the choice of amino acids may have been optimized by evolution. Alien life that began using a different set of amino acids might then have evolved over time to adopt the same set that familiar life-forms use.

The difficulty of determining whether a creature is alien is exacerbated by the fact that there are two competing theories of biogenesis. The first is that life begins with an abrupt and distinctive transformation, akin to a phase transition in physics, perhaps triggered when a system reaches a certain threshold of chemical complexity. The system need not be a single cell. Biologists have proposed that primitive life emerged from a community of cells that traded material and information and that cellular autonomy and species individuation came later. The alternative view is that there is a smooth, extended continuum from chemistry to biology, with no clear line of demarcation that can be identified as the genesis of life.

If life, so famously problematic to define, is said to be a system having a property–such as the ability to store and process certain kinds of information–that marks a well-defined transition from the nonliving to the living realm, it would be meaningful to talk about one or more origin-of-life events. If, however, life is weakly defined as something like organized complexity, the roots of life may meld seamlessly into the realm of general complex chemistry. It would then be a formidable task to demonstrate independent origins for different forms of life unless the two types of organisms were so widely separated that they could not have come into contact (for instance, if they were located on planets in different star systems).

It is clear that we have sampled only a tiny fraction of Earth's microbial population. Each discovery has brought surprises and forced us to expand our notion of what is biologically possible. As more terrestrial environments are explored, it seems very likely that new and ever more exotic forms of life will be discovered. If this search were to uncover evidence for a second genesis, it would strongly support the theory that life is a cosmic phenomenon and lend credence to the belief that we are not alone in the universe.

About the Author

Paul Davies is a theoretical physicist, cosmologist and astrobiologist. He is currently director of Beyond, a research center at Arizona State University devoted to exploring the big questions of science. Davies is the author or co-author of 27 books; his latest work is Cosmic Jackpot: Why Our Universe Is Just Right for Life *(Houghton Mifflin, 2007).*

Section 2: Searching for Signs of Life

Life Is Complicated—Literally, Astrobiologists Say

By Natalie Elliot

The hunt for extraterrestrial life has always been bedeviled by false positives—those occasions where scientists think they've found life but turn out to lack a wholly convincing case.

The archetypal example comes from NASA's twin *Viking* landers, which delivered controversial evidence of life on Mars in the mid-1970s. That evidence was a whiff of radioactive carbon wafting from Martian soil, hinting at microbial metabolism taking place within—but three other life-detection experiments each lander carried only found null results. More muddled data about life on Mars arrived in 1996, when scientists discovered what could have been microbial microfossils inside a Martian meteorite found in Antarctica. But subsequent studies showed the putative microfossils could have easily been produced by several other entirely abiotic routes. Most recently, researchers studying the atmosphere of Venus claimed to see significant amounts of phosphine there—a gas that, on Earth, is chiefly made by microorganisms. Yet soon other scientists had cast doubt on the validity of those measurements, and had postulated the gas—if it was there at all—was from some strange-but-lifeless form of Venusian volcanism.

In each case, the pattern was the same: initial excitement, followed by subsequent skepticism, and eventual dismissal. Time and time again, it seems, astrobiologists are only finding alien signs of life—so-called biosignatures—that are frustratingly inconclusive. This is in large part because astrobiologists by necessity seek the simplest, most robust forms of life that appear possible in harsh otherworldly environments, and the chemicals and structures we often associate with such organisms on Earth can often be produced abiotically. And, of course, the chemistry of alien life might be entirely different from what we observe on our own planet. Is there a better way to look?

A new theory published in *Nature Communications* contends that there is. Called assembly theory, it turns away from the search for simple chemical biosignatures, instead embracing life's fundamental complexity. It is based on the idea that any form of biology anywhere in the universe will encode life's information in complex assemblages of molecules that are measurably distinct from lifeless matter.

For study co-author Sara Walker, a biophysicist at Arizona State University, assembly theory is a landmark for the field, because it "presents the first complexity measure that is testable in the lab." More broadly, she says, it gives us "the first glimmer of our ability to connect deep theoretical ideas about the nature of life to empirical observables."

In astrobiology, appeals to complexity have been on the rise for a while now. In light of the ambiguous results that can come from research focused on simple chemical signatures, scientists have developed theories and definitions of life that look to more sophisticated processes–metabolism, adaptation, replication, evolution–that could help us distinguish living systems from nonliving ones. In 1994, for example, NASA adopted a complex definition of life: "Life is a self-sustaining chemical system capable of Darwinian evolution." The trouble is, the key concepts behind such advanced frameworks are themselves complicated, making them notoriously difficult to test and quantify. Ask, for instance, five different evolutionary biologists for their working definition of "Darwinian evolution," and you are likely to get five slightly different answers. As NASA's chief scientist, Jim Green, explains, "I can't build an instrument that is going to go out and find 'evolution,' 'reproduction,' or 'metabolism.'"

Assembly theory may offer a clearer, more general way to recognize life, whether familiar or alien. It builds on two related ideas: physical complexity and abundance, positing that as these two properties increase for any given object in any given environment, the chances of an abiotic origin decrease. Abundance tracks how often an object appears in an environment, whereas an object's complexity is measured by estimating the number of steps required for its assembly. Consider the difference between a seashore littered with water-worn pebbles—a situation that could easily be ascribed to a lifeless process—and one strewn instead with intricately sculpted seashells.

Although the theory is general and can pertain to many kinds of objects across a wide range of scales, the researchers looked at how it applies to molecules, arguably the most essential building blocks of biology that scientists can seek both in the lab and in space.

To rank molecular complexity, the team created a mass assembly index, which algorithmically assigns a mass assembly number (MA) to different kinds of molecules. As a proof of concept, they used this approach to index and rank 2.5 million molecules in a widely used chemistry database. A molecule with an MA of 1 has low complexity and thus a higher chance of abiotic origins; more complex molecules are assigned higher numbers. Composed of one atom of phosphorus and three atoms of hydrogen, phosphine gas—the putative Venusian biosignature—only merits an MA of 1. In contrast, the amino acid tryptophan earns an MA of 12 thanks to its elaborate structure of 11 carbon atoms, twelve of hydrogen, and a pair apiece of nitrogen and oxygen.

According to Lee Cronin, a chemist at the University of Glasgow who led the research, this exercise revealed that at a certain threshold—circa MA 15—a molecule's probability of abiotic production in Earth-like conditions becomes astronomically low. Less than one in about 600 sextillion, in fact, Cronin says. Thus, molecules ranking at an MA of 15 or higher should almost always be made by life.

So, does that mean that MA 15 is the surefire marker for life everywhere? No. For one thing, many low-ranking molecules can be biosignatures—such as the structurally simple molecular oxygen emitted into Earth's atmosphere by photosynthetic organisms. This means that, although it may decrease the chances of false positives in the search for life, assembly theory also correspondingly raises the likelihood of "false negatives" allowing genuine biosignatures to slip through investigative cracks. More broadly, Cronin says, although MA 15 seems to be the threshold value for life on Earth, the threshold could fall elsewhere for wildly different planetary environments. The trick, Cronin argues, is to use assembly theory to map the gap that must exist between the chemical combinations produced abiotically and those produced by living systems—here or anywhere else.

To further validate their approach, Cronin and colleagues double-checked their theoretical calculations of complexity by using mass spectrometry fragmentation to study a large sample of ranked molecules and substances, breaking each down into its constituent parts to confirm the number of chemical steps required to reassemble them. Those experimental results hewed closely to theoretical predictions, and reliably distinguished between a broad range of living, nonliving, and dead substances, including *E. coli* bacteria, yeast cells, plant alkaloids, ashes, coal, granite, limestone, and even beer.

One of the most exciting validations came courtesy of Cronin's collaborator and study co-author Heather Graham, an astrobiologist at NASA's Goddard Space Flight Center in Greenbelt, Md. To conduct a test of the theory, Graham's lab sent a set of blind samples. One of these was preserved biological material from a multimillion-year-old fossil. Another was a sample from the Murchison meteorite, a bolide rich in organic (but abiotic) carbon compounds that fell to Earth in 1969. Cronin's testing flagged the Murchison material as notable for its wealth of complex molecules but still ranked it as below the threshold of MA 15 and thus lifeless. The fossil material, however, was identified as a signature of life.

For study co-author and NASA astrobiology postdoctoral fellow Cole Mathis, there was a striking moment at this stage of the research when a significant distinction became clear to all involved: the distinction between "a complex sample and a complex molecule." While a strange variety of chemicals like those present in Murchison might lead one to think that something like life was present there, it is actually the complex molecule, which indicates the organization of chemistry, that seems to be key to life.

The success of these results, and the publication of the work, brought out initial excitement. Steven Benner, a chemist at the Foundation for Applied Molecular Evolution in Alachua, Fla., who was not part of the research, says he and his colleagues are "extremely enthusiastic" about assembly theory. Even so, he adds, Cronin and colleagues still must address many unanswered questions about their work, especially whether it could actually be applied in "truly exotic environments." Benner has challenged Cronin to test the approach on samples of "semi-complex" material that Benner's group has synthesized from simple carbon precursors in lab conditions mimicking the atmosphere of Venus. "This is a real environment," Benner says, "one soon to be visited in a space mission again. If Venusian life exists in the clouds above Venus, it would need to follow a chemical logic very much different from the logic that is followed by life on Earth." This, Benner says, arguably makes Venus the best site for a near-term test of the molecular-complexity metric.

In response, Cronin has remarked that Benner's samples pose a particular challenge, as they are immersed in sulfuric acid–which decomposes organic molecules and thus lowers their detectable organic complexity. Nevertheless, Cronin says, "we are working on a way to reconstruct that complexity, so I remain hopeful that even in the most difficult samples, if the molecule is not broken, we can take a measurement."

In the meantime, Green and others at NASA have wondered whether assembly theory might be used to analyze data from the many mass spectrometers that have visited other worlds during the agency's various interplanetary missions. Green first considered the case of the mass spectrometer on the *Cassini* orbiter, which flew through and sampled plumes of water vapor venting from Saturn's icy moon Enceladus, but he realized that *Cassini's* instrument only registered masses up to 100 atomic mass units (amu), and assembly theory only works for molecules weighing at least 150 amu.

Although they could reach 150 amu and beyond, instruments on the Curiosity and Perseverance Mars rovers fell short, too, lacking the specificity to study single molecular species for an MA measurement. Future missions, Green says, should all be equipped with mass spectrometers that register the higher mass and take measurements with greater specification. There is promise for NASA's Dragonfly mission, a nuclear-powered quadcopter slated to begin exploring the atmosphere and surface of Saturn's moon Titan in the mid-2030s. Graham points out that Dragonfly's mass spectrometer, though it lacks some of the capabilities of lab spectrometers, will have the capacity to detect complex molecules.

In the future, other planned missions could seek out signs of life's molecular complexity at astrobiological hot spots across the solar system. Eventually, Cronin speculates, assembly theory might even be used to assess potential biosignatures remotely detected in the atmospheres of potentially habitable exoplanets by large telescopes.

For now, however, the approach has given theorists and experimentalists alike a wealth of new ideas for understanding–and seeing–life's cosmic complexity.

About the Author

Natalie Elliot is a science writer who writes about the origin of life, astrobiology, and the history of science. She teaches classics and history of science at St. John's College. Her work has appeared in Aeon *and* The New Atlantis.

Hardy Microbes Hint at Possibilities for Extraterrestrial Life

By Brianne Palmer

"I am very sure that there is life up there, somewhere in our solar system," says Christine Moissl-Eichinger, a microbiologist at the Medical University of Graz in Austria. But like any scientist, Moissl-Eichinger knows full well that substantial proof is needed for such a substantial claim. So she and others are working to find that proof–both here on Earth and on Mars.

On the Red Planet, NASA's Mars rover Perseverance is searching for fossils and traces of alien biochemistry in Jezero Crater, an ancient lake bed thought to have once offered habitable conditions for microbial life. Back home, microbiologists are investigating oxygen-poor environments that may mimic the habitat of early Mars. This two-pronged approach of grounding scientists' extraterrestrial extrapolations with studies of Earthly analogues could help clarify the bedrock limits for life on rocky planets, greatly aiding the development and execution of future extraterrestrial missions.

The Mars Analogues for Space Exploration project (MASE) was a four-year-long effort that used Earth to understand Mars by analyzing five types of harsh but habitable terrestrial environments that may resemble those that once–or even now–exist on our neighboring planet. Its funding concluded in 2017, but MASE researchers continue to publish results about the habitability of Mars. The study sites included a sulfidic spring, a briny mine, an acidic lake and river, and permafrost. Because of the extreme conditions in these environments, organisms that live here are called extremophiles.

Extremophile research was pioneered by the late Thomas Brock, a microbiologist at the University of Wisconsin–Madison. He found, against all expectations, that certain hardy microbes could thrive in geothermal springs hot enough to poach an egg. The microbiologist's curiosity led to the isolation of a molecule–from a heat-loving bacterium—that is now used in labs across the world to amplify and sequence DNA. Brock passed away in April, but his legacy lives on.

Brock published his extremophile findings in April 1969, mere months before humans first walked on the moon. This paved the way for astrobiology, the study of life in all its forms on this planet and elsewhere in the universe. Astrobiology is not about making money off of space travel, says Luke McKay, a researcher at Montana State University, who was not involved with that study or Moissl-Eichinger's recent research. It is about basic science and answering a single, timeless question: Does life exist beyond Earth?

This is a question so profound that so far scientists have only managed to chip away at its edges, with each hard-won revelation usually accompanied by a host of newfound mysteries. Moissl-Eichinger and her team's chief contribution has been their attempt at cultivating extremophiles from MASE's five environments, but even this straightforward task has been devilishly difficult. Out of more than 1,000 different extremophile species gathered from those sites, the team managed to grow just 31 in the lab. This is a common struggle in environmental microbiology. Because these microbes live in extreme places, it is difficult for researchers to re-create the exact conditions they require to thrive. To capture more of the diversity, the team's scientists used genetic sequencing, which allowed them to look at all the microbial DNA in their samples. They specifically searched for genes that may help microbes survive hostile conditions, such as extreme temperatures or the absence of oxygen.

"Cultured [microbial] isolates are not representative of the environment, and that's why it's really cool what they did. By using isolates and sequencing, I think they really tried to cover all the bases," McKay says.

Despite their trouble culturing their extremophile samples, the researchers discovered a vast diversity of microorganisms in all five locations. Even in the most extreme Earthly environments, it seems, life indeed finds a way. Most remarkably, the team's DNA sequencing revealed 34 unique microbial sequences that were conserved in all

MASE sites, which is evidence of microbes surviving a combination of extreme environments. According to Moissl-Eichinger, while many microbes are adapted to live in certain conditions such as intense cold or scant oxygen, it is novel to find a group of microbes adapted to survive a combination of these extreme stressors. This ability to survive many types of environments strengthens the researchers' claims that similar microbes could exist on Mars—not only in the deep past but even today.

"Microbes are everywhere. They can live in places where we'd expect they could not thrive, but somehow they do," Moissl-Eichinger says. "Of course, on Mars, we do not know if these [extremophiles] are the types of microorganisms we expect to see. They may just be very adapted to life on Earth."

One way these microbes may be particularly adapted to life on Earth is their dependence on carbon-based compounds, or organic matter. These are the molecular building blocks of life on Earth and may be rare in some otherwise-habitable extraterrestrial environments. Some microbes in environments with scarce organic matter can instead get nutrients from inorganic substances, such as ammonia and certain sulfur compounds. Yet all the microbes cultured in the MASE studies relied on organic carbon to survive—even those that could survive without oxygen. According to Moissl-Eichinger, this could be because microbes that consume organic matter grow faster. So with more time, she and her colleagues might successfully culture microbes that get their nutrients from other chemical sources, potentially revealing new biochemical pathways and ecological niches to consider when searching for life on Mars.

"We are far away from understanding what microbes could look like on Mars and how we can find them. But of course, research always gives a little piece by piece, and at some point, the picture gets fuller," Moissl-Eichinger says.

Understanding how all these disparate pieces fit together may change our definition of what it means to be alive. According to McKay, extraterrestrial environments for life may be like those found on Earth, or they could differ vastly. At present, given our sample size of only one confirmed life-bearing world, both possibilities appear equally plausible.

"If [extraterrestrial life] is too [similar] to our life on Earth, people will argue that it is something that we brought with us. But if it is too different, will we be able to see it?" says Moissel-Eichinger, "Now that is the question that drives us."

About the Author

Brianne Palmer is a PhD student at San Diego State University and the University of California, Davis studying how soil microbes respond to fire. She frequently writes about the intersection of technology and the environment.

How to Search for Life on Mars

By Christopher P. McKay, Victor Parro García

Astronomers have learned a great many things about Mars since the first probes landed there nearly four decades ago.

We know that liquid water once flowed across its surface and that Mars and Earth were similar in their early history. When life on Earth arose, some 3.5 billion years ago, Mars was warmer than it is today and had liquid oceans, an active magnetic field, and a thicker atmosphere. Given the similarity between the two planets, it seems reasonable to think that whatever steps led to life on Earth could also have occurred on Mars.

In fact, for all we know, microscopic life might still exist on the Red Planet. Every mission to our neighbor in the past 35 years has examined its geology, not its biology. Only the twin *Viking 1* and *2* spacecraft, which touched down in 1976, conducted the first and thus far only search for life on another world. Each spacecraft carried four experiments relevant to the search, and each experiment returned ambiguous data. The Viking missions gave us puzzles, not answers. Yet we now know that the Viking methods would not have been able to find life on Mars even if it were there–which means the question of whether the planet harbors life remains open.

Fortunately, in the intervening decades microbiologists have developed a cornucopia of tools for detecting microorganisms. These tools are now unexceptional here on Earth. But if applied by one of the several missions soon expected to head for Mars, they could deliver a first: a definitive answer as to whether our closest neighbor also pulses with life.

The First Search

The Viking experiments looked for life using standard search techniques of the time. In the initial experiment, the lander took a scoop of Martian soil and added carbon compounds as food for any microorganisms that might be in the soil. If microbes did exist in the soil, we might expect them to consume the food and release carbon dioxide.

In fact, the Viking missions did see this behavior. On its own, the test would seem to indicate that microorganisms were present in the Martian soil. When combined with the results of the other experiments, however, researchers could not be sure.

The second experiment looked for evidence of photosynthesis but returned inconclusive results. A third experiment added water into a soil sample. If life were present, the moist soil might have produced carbon dioxide. Instead it produced oxygen. This was very strange, as no known soil on Earth does this. Scientists concluded that the oxygen came from a chemical reaction.

In the final experiment, the landers searched for organic compounds in the soil. Organics are carbon-containing compounds that form the building blocks of life. If any life existed on Mars, we would expect to find these compounds. Yet organics alone would not provide definitive evidence of life, because we also expect meteorites to continuously deposit organic compounds on Mars. Puzzlingly, the experiment found no evidence of organics whatsoever.

Taken together, the findings left investigators stumped. Most scientists believed that chemical reactions were responsible for the results in the last two experiments, but chemistry could not quite explain the first. A small but vocal minority of Mars scientists held that the first experiment did, in fact, find evidence of life. But most everyone else concluded that Mars was barren.

In 2008, 32 years after *Viking 1* and *2* landed, the solution to these puzzles began to emerge when NASA's *Phoenix* lander touched down in the northern polar region of Mars. To everyone's surprise, *Phoenix* detected perchlorate, a rare molecule on Earth that features four oxygen atoms connected to a chlorine ion, which are connected to a magnesium or calcium ion. When perchlorate salts reach 350 degrees Celsius, they decompose, releasing reactive oxygen and chlorine. Perchlorates are so reactive that they are used in many rocket fuels.

This finding made investigators see that the perchlorates could well have obliterated signs of life in the soil. The Viking mission's organic search experiment first heated the soil sample to 500 degrees C so that it might vaporize any organic molecules and detect them in gaseous form. But in 2010 a team led by Rafael Navarro-González of the National Autonomous University of Mexico, which included one of us (McKay), showed that perchlorate would have completely destroyed any carbon compounds in the soil during the heating process.

Perchlorate also illuminates the puzzles of the first and third experiments. In the first experiment, adding food to the soil generated carbon dioxide. But perchlorate produces bleachlike compounds when exposed to cosmic rays. These compounds can decompose organic molecules (such as those found in the added food), producing carbon dioxide in the process. In the third experiment, oxygen emerged from moistened soil. The perchlorate bleach production also forms oxygen, yet the oxygen remains initially trapped in the soil. It is released only later, once the soil is wetted, as happened with the Viking mission. Two mysteries solved.

Yet hope for the discovery of life is not lost. The Curiosity rover landed on Mars in 2012 and has been taking samples of the soil ever since. In early 2014 the Sample Analysis at Mars (SAM) instrument team (which includes McKay), led by Paul Mahaffy of NASA's Goddard Space Flight Center, reported that the experiment found carbon compounds in ancient mudstone sediments on the bottom of Gale Crater, even in the presence of perchlorate. Later, in 2015, the SAM team reported the presence of chlorobenzene in one of the Martian samples. Complex organics exist on Mars–the Viking mission was just unable to find them. Could the same be true for life itself?

Modern Approaches

In the 40 years since *Viking 1* and *2* landers were built, microbiology technology has changed dramatically. The Viking missions used culture-based methods, in which microorganisms grow in petri dishes. But these are no longer considered definitive, and we now know that only a small fraction of soil microbes can be cultured. Scientists have developed vastly more sensitive techniques that directly detect the biomolecules in microbial life-forms. These new methods provide the basis for a novel way to search for evidence of life on Mars.

The most widely known method is DNA detection and sequencing. No longer is it necessary to culture an organism so that it will replicate sufficiently to provide enough DNA for sequencing. Several teams are working on ways to incorporate DNA-extraction technologies into instruments suitable for upcoming Mars missions.

One drawback of relying on DNA detection to reveal life on Mars is that although DNA is common to all life on Earth, it may not occur in alien life. Or if it is present, it may be so different that DNA detectors built to find Earth biology will miss it.

Fortunately, Mars could harbor other signs of life. Among these biomarkers are proteins and polysaccharides. Proteins are long, linear chains composed of various mixtures of the 20 different kinds of amino acids used by life. Amino acids are present in meteorites and are likely to have been a common component of the prebiotic environment on any world. Polysaccharides are long chains of sugars constructed by enzymes (biological catalysts), which themselves are proteins.

Detecting molecules as complex as a protein or a polysaccharide would be strong evidence of life, widely defined: a biological system that encodes information and uses this information to build complex molecules. These complex molecules would stand out against any background of simple prebiotic molecules like a skyscraper would stand out against a field of boulders.

One of us (Parro García) has been developing an instrument for detecting such complex molecules on Mars. It is based on a technique–immunoassay testing–already in use for simultaneously detecting hundreds of different types of proteins, polysaccharides, and other biomolecules (including DNA itself).

Immunoassay tests employ antibodies–Y-shaped proteins–each of which binds to just one type of biomolecule. In an immunoassay test, a solution that might contain substances of interest is poured over a large array of antibodies, each one designed to bind to a specific target. If the sample solution contains a biomolecule that links to an antibody in the array, the antibody will capture and, by binding, identify it.

One nice feature of immunoassays is that antibodies can detect molecules that are smaller and less complex than full proteins are. The test can thus search for molecules that are life-related but of lesser complexity, such as fragments of proteins that have broken into bits. Finding these bits would also imply that life exists.

All of Earth's organisms collectively contain many millions of different proteins. With so many to choose from, how do we pick the few hundred that a single immunoassay test could search for? The short answer is that we cannot know for sure. But we can make educated guesses based on two strategies: First, we could search for proteins that would be useful or essential to survival on Mars. For example, we might search for enzymes that consume perchlorate, cold-adapted enzymes that would allow a microorganism to survive Mars's frigid temperatures or enzymes that would repair damage to DNA caused by Mars's strong ionizing radiation. Second, we could target molecules that are ubiquitous throughout the microbial world, such as peptidoglycan, which is a universal component of all bacterial cell walls, or adenosine triphosphate (ATP), which is used by all living organisms on Earth to transport chemical energy for metabolic activity.

Even if Mars's harsh environment has destroyed large molecules such as DNA and proteins, we might still find evidence for life in the debris. Many types of molecules are chemically equivalent to one another but may have opposite "chirality"–their bonds may twist to the left or the right. Life on Earth is dominated by left-handed amino acids. If an experiment detects amino acids and finds a particular set that has a dominant left- or right-handed chirality, this would be compelling evidence for the presence of life. Interestingly, if that chirality were right-handed–the opposite of Earth proteins–it would be evidence that the life-forms on Mars evolved independently from life on Earth.

Mission Planning

The Viking missions carried three biology experiments; we might imagine a mission to Mars that also carries three biomarker search instruments–perhaps a DNA detector, an immunoassay microchip, and an instrument to detect and characterize amino acids. The technology is nearly ready. The next task is to pick a target–the location that holds the best chance of harboring biomarkers.

Ice and salt are friends to biomarkers, protecting them from damage and decay. The enemies? Ionizing radiation and heat. Fortunately, the low temperatures on Mars make thermal decay negligible even over the age of the planet. Ionizing radiation, however, could completely destroy biomarkers that are within the first meter or so of the surface over a few billion years. The promising targets, then, are icy sites that may have harbored recent life–such as the Phoenix landing site near Mars's north pole–or sites where erosion has recently exposed the ancient material. In either case, one would want to drill down to extract samples from a meter or more below the surface.

The missions to Mars that are now being planned could conduct this search. The European ExoMars mission, slated for 2020, should be able to carry a drill. NASA is working on a mission that will launch another copy of the Curiosity rover in 2020. ExoMars and the new Curiosity could search the dry equatorial regions of Mars for biomarkers in salt and sedimentary deposits. (Neither rover can function in the polar regions.)

As for a polar search, NASA is studying an inexpensive lander called Icebreaker that could do the job. Equipped with a one-meter drill and an immunoassay instrument, it could search the water-rich northern permafrost of Mars for biomarkers in the ice-cemented ground.

Any one of these missions would be a worthy candidate to lead the next era of Mars exploration. The past few decades of research have left no doubt that Mars once harbored liquid water. The time has now come to test whether that once watery planet provided a home to any life-forms. If we find biological molecules on Mars—and especially if those molecules indicate that Martian life arose independently of Earth life—we will gain a profound insight into life beyond our home. Just as we know that there are many stars and many planets, we will know that there are many biologies. We will know that the universe is alive with diversity.

About the Authors

Christopher P. McKay is a scientist at NASA's Ames Research Center.

Victor Parro García is a scientist at the Center for Astrobiology in Spain.

New Approach Could Boost the Search for Life in Otherworldly Oceans

By Natalie Elliot

The hottest spots in the search for alien life are a few frigid moons in the outer solar system, each known to harbor a liquid water ocean beneath its icy exterior. There is Saturn's moon Titan, which hides a thick layer of briny water beneath a frozen surface dotted with lakes of liquid hydrocarbon. Titan's sister Saturnian moon Enceladus has revealed its subsurface sea with geyserlike plumes venting from cracks near its south pole. Plumes also emanate from a moon that is one planet closer to the sun: Jupiter's Europa, which boasts a watery deep so vast that, by volume, it dwarfs all of Earth's oceans combined. Each of these aquatic extraterrestrial locales might be the site of a "second genesis," an emergence of life of the same sort that occurred on Earth billions of years ago.

Astrobiologists are now pursuing multiple interplanetary missions to learn whether any of these ocean-bearing moons actually possess more than mere water–namely, habitability, or the nuanced geochemical conditions required for life to arise and flourish. NASA's instrument-packed *Europa Clipper* spacecraft, for example, could begin its orbital investigations of Jupiter's enigmatic moon by 2030. And another mission called Dragonfly, using a nuclear-fueled flying drone, is scheduled to touch down on Titan as early as 2036. As impressive as these missions are, however, they are only preludes to future efforts that could more directly hunt for alien life itself. But in those strange sunless places so unlike our own world, how will astrobiologists know life when they see it?

More often than not, the "biosignatures" scientists look for in such searches are subtle chemical tracers of life's past or current presence on a planet rather than anything so obvious as a fossilized form protruding from a rock or a little green humanoid waving hello. The instruments on NASA's Perseverance Mars rover, for instance, can detect organic compounds and salts in and around its landing site: Jezero Crater, a dry lakebed that may contain evidence of past life. And in the fall of 2020 some astronomers telescopically studying Venus may have teased out the presence of phosphine gas there, a possible by-product of putative microbes floating in temperate regions of the planet's atmosphere.

The trouble is that many simple biosignatures can be produced both by living things and through abiotic geochemical processes. Much of the phosphine on Earth comes from microbes, but Venus's phosphine, if it exists at all, could potentially be linked to erupting volcanoes rather than some alien ecosystem in its clouds. Such ambiguities can lead to false positives, cases in which scientists think they see life where none exists. At the same time, if organisms possess radically different biochemistry and physiology from that of terrestrial creatures, scientists could instead encounter false negatives, cases in which they do not recognize life despite having evidence for its presence. Especially when contemplating prospects for life on distinctly alien worlds such as the ocean moons of the outer solar system, researchers must carefully navigate between these two interlinked hazards–the Scylla and Charybdis of astrobiology.

Now, however, a study recently published in the Bulletin of Mathematical Biology offers a novel approach. By shifting attention from specific chemical tracers–such as phosphine–to the broader question of how biological processes reorganize materials across entire ecosystems, the paper's authors say, astrobiologists could illuminate new types of less ambiguous biosignatures. These clues would be suitable for discovering life in its myriad possible forms–even if that life employed profoundly unearthly biochemistry.

Sizing Up a Sea Change

The study relies on stoichiometry, which measures the elemental ratios that appear in the chemistry of cells and ecosystems. The researchers began with the observation that within groups of cells, chemical ratios vary with striking regularity. The classic example of this regularity is the Redfield ratio—a 16:1 average proportion of nitrogen to phosphorus displayed with remarkable consistency by phytoplankton blooms throughout Earth's oceans. Other kinds of cells, such as certain types of bacteria, also exhibit their own characteristically consistent ratios. If the regularity of chemical ratios within cells is a universal property of biological systems, here or anywhere else in the cosmos, then careful stoichiometry could be the key to eventually discovering life on an alien world.

Importantly, however, these elemental proportions change in accordance with cell size, allowing for an additional check on any curiously consistent but possibly abiotic chemical ratios on another world. In bacteria, for instance, as cells get larger, concentrations of protein molecules decrease, whereas concentrations of nucleic acids increase. In contrast to groups of nonliving particles, biological particles will display "ratios that systematically change with cell size," explains Santa Fe Institute researcher Chris Kempes, who led the new study, which expanded on prior work by co-author Simon Levin, also at the Santa Fe Institute. The trick is to devise a general theory of how, exactly, the various sizes of cells affect elemental abundances—which is precisely what Kempes, Levin, and their colleagues did.

They focused on the fact that, at least for Earth life, as cell sizes increase in a fluid, their abundance decreases in a mathematically patterned way—specifically, as a power law, the rate of which can be expressed by a negative exponent. This suggests that, if astrobiologists know the size distribution of cells (or cell-like particles) in a fluid, they can predict the elemental abundances within those materials. In essence, this could be a potent recipe for determining whether a group of unknown particles, say within a sample of Europan seawater, harbors anything alive. "If we observe a system where we have particles with systematic relationships between elemental ratios and size, and the surrounding fluid does not contain these ratios," Kempes explains, "we have a strong signal that the ecosystem may contain life."

Testing the Waters

The study's emphasis on such "ecological biosignatures" is the latest in a slow-simmering, decades-long quest to link life not only to the fundamental limitations of physics and chemistry but also to the specific environments in which it appears. It would, after all, be somewhat naive to assume organisms on the sunbathed surface of a warm, rocky planet would have the very same chemical biosignatures as those dwelling within the lightless depths of an oceanic moon. "There has been a constant evolution in ideas, in approaches, and that's really important," explains Jim Green, NASA's chief scientist, who was not involved in the new study. "Now we are entering an era where we can go after what we know about how life has evolved and apply that as a general principle."

So what does it take to bring this more holistic approach to biosignatures to our studies of worlds such as Europa, Titan, and Enceladus? At the moment, Green explains, it will take more than the space agency's *Europa Clipper* orbiter–perhaps a follow-up mission to the surface would suffice. "Through *Clipper*, we want to take much more detailed measurements, fly through the plume, study the evolution of Europa over a period of time and capture high-resolution images," he says. "This would take us to the next step, which would be to get down to the ground. That's where the next generation of ideas and instruments need to come in."

Looking for the ecological biosignatures described by Kempes and his colleagues would require instrumentation that measures the size distribution and chemical composition of cells within their native fluid. On Earth, the technique that scientists use to sort cells by size is called flow cytometry, and it is used frequently in marine environments. But performing cytometry in an alien moon's subsurface ocean would be far more challenging than merely sending instrumentation there: Because of the paucity of available energy in those sunlight-starved abysses, scientists expect any life there to be single-celled, extremely small, and relatively sparse. To capture such organisms in the first place would require careful filtering and then a refined flow cytometer that would measure particles of this size range.

Our current flow cytometers are not up to that task, explains Sarah Maurer, a biochemist and astrobiologist at Central Connecticut University, who was not involved with the study. Many kinds of cells simply do not get picked up, and "there are cell types that require extensive preparation or they won't go through a cytometer," she says. To work in space, instruments to filter and sort cells would need both refinement on Earth and miniaturization for spaceflight.

Progress is already being made on both fronts, according to study co-author Heather Graham of the NASA-funded Laboratory for Agnostic Biosignatures and the agency's Goddard Space Flight Center. The next steps, she says, will be to deploy new tools at marginally habitable field sites around the globe that play host to some of Earth's most extreme and impoverished ecosystems. Once astrobiologists begin routinely discerning the distinctive chemical ratios associated with living ecosystems in our own planet's quiescent waters, they can fine-tune the specifications for spaceflight-capable devices–and, just maybe, at last reveal a second genesis, written within the mathematics of a subsurface ocean's chemistry.

About the Author

Natalie Elliot is a science writer who writes about the origin of life, astrobiology, and the history of science. She teaches classics and history of science at St. John's College. Her work has appeared in Aeon *and* The New Atlantis.

Hunt for Alien Life Tops Next-Gen Wish List for U.S. Astronomy

By Lee Billings

About 20 years from now, astronomers will be in the midst of a revolutionary era of discovery, using new telescopes on the ground and in space to study the cradle-to-grave evolution of galaxies, probe the deepest origins of black holes, glimpse the earliest moments of cosmic time, and gather breakthrough images of Earth-like worlds orbiting other stars. And on average, those future researchers should also be healthier and happier, more diverse and inclusive, than their present-day counterparts.

At least, that is the plan, according to the long-awaited major report "Pathways to Discovery in Astronomy and Astrophysics for the 2020s." Also known as Astro2020, the report is the seventh iteration of a once-every-10-years "Decadal Survey" process for astronomy conducted by the National Academies of Sciences, Engineering, and Medicine. Its overarching purpose is twofold: to codify communal consensus on the future of the field via a ranked list of research priorities and, perhaps more importantly, to muster vigorous support from federal policy makers for sustaining the broader enterprise of U.S. astronomy.

In pursuit of those goals, this latest Decadal Survey deviates sharply from its predecessors, which traditionally reserved their highest recommendations for specific new telescopes that were tightly bound to a small slice of the electromagnetic spectrum. Instead Astro2020's highest space-based recommendation envisions a fundamental shift in the way that NASA plans and develops large, multibillion-dollar "flagship" astronomy projects. Dubbed the Great Observatories Mission and Technology Maturation Program, the initiative would invest $1.2 billion in the 2020s toward key enabling technologies for multiple proposed facilities in hopes of lowering the overall cost and risk associated with building and launching an entire fleet of next-generation telescopes to work together across a wide range of wavelengths, from infrared to x-rays.

The need for better management of NASA's future astrophysical megaprojects is particularly urgent, given missteps in handling those of the present and recent past. The James Webb Space Telescope–the top flagship recommendation of the first Decadal Survey of the new millennium–is only now reaching the launchpad after a series of near-catastrophic multibillion-dollar budget overruns and agonizing schedule slips. The top recommendation from the Decadal Survey of 2010, the Nancy Grace Roman Space Telescope, has fared better but has still suffered costly setbacks that delayed its launch until circa 2027.

The premier result of Astro2020's top-recommended new program would be a supersize and far more sophisticated successor to the Hubble Space Telescope, which itself was the first in NASA's sequence of four "Great Observatories" sent aloft between 1990 and 2003. Like Hubble, it would operate in optical, infrared, and ultraviolet wavelengths, but it would be perhaps three times larger than that storied observatory and built for an estimated $11 billion. Beginning development at the end of this decade for a notional launch in the mid-2040s, it would snap pictures of dozens of potentially habitable exoplanets and study their atmospheres for signs of life while also being a workhorse for a wealth of transformative astrophysics. Although it has no catchy formal name as of yet, astronomers are already referring to this project as "LuvEx," referencing two progenitor telescope concepts–LUVOIR (Large Ultraviolet Optical Infrared Surveyor) and HabEx (Habitable Exoplanet Observatory)–that fed into its creation. In short order, it would be followed by two additional facilities, one focused on the far-infrared and the other on x-rays, each built for a projected cost of $3 billion to $5 billion. These follow-on facilities also reflect two preexisting proposals: the far-infrared Origins telescope and the Lynx X-ray Observatory.

A Bright Future

"This report sets an ambitious, inspirational, and aspirational vision for the coming decade of astronomy and astrophysics," said Fiona Harrison, a California Institute of Technology astronomer and co-chair of the Astro2020 steering committee, in a statement. "In changing how we plan for the most ambitious strategic space projects, we can develop a broad portfolio of missions to pursue visionary goals, such as searching for life on planets orbiting stars in our galactic neighborhood–and at the same time exploit the richness of 21st-century astrophysics through a panchromatic fleet."

Many astronomers are understandably ecstatic. "I believe this is the smartest, most executable and pragmatic Decadal Survey ever written," says John O'Meara, a vocal champion of the LUVOIR concept and chief scientist of the W. M. Keck Observatory on Mauna Kea in Hawaii. "The steering committee understood that we must redefine how we develop large missions so that we can realize this vision of new Great Observatories. They have brilliantly laid out how to achieve civilization-changing science in an uncertain world, and I hope NASA and other federal agencies embrace the spirit of the document."

"We stand at the threshold of a new golden era of discovery," says Heidi Hammel, vice president for science at the Association of Universities for Research in Astronomy. "Might we actually find evidence for life on another planet? This report, true to its name, lays out robust pathways to answer this question, and we can be the generation that answers it!"

Marc Postman, a distinguished astronomer at the Space Telescope Science Institute and a long-time proponent of large exoplanet-imaging observatories, holds a somewhat longer but no less gleeful view. "I'm walking on air right now because this is the culmination of a personal 15-year journey to get to this point. People ask me why I've spent time on this, because, when [LuvEx] launches, I will certainly be retired but hopefully still in my mortal shell. I tell them I'm doing this for the future even if I never use it or see it get off the ground. And based on this Astro2020 report, the future is very bright. This is a generational initiative that is beyond any individual. Humanity is about to truly embark on a quest to learn whether we are alone in the universe."

Besides the big-ticket item of a life-hunting telescope as the first of a line of flagship Great Observatories, Astro2020's space-based recommendations also call for new once-per-decade "probe-class" missions with $1.5 billion cost caps, as well as significant spending to enhance astronomers' abilities to study split-second celestial phenomena in real time using not only light but subatomic particles and gravitational waves as well.

Astro2020's purview also extends to U.S. ground-based projects, which are typically funded and managed by the National Science Foundation (NSF) or occasionally by the Department of Energy. In this category, the report gives top ranking to a program to invest some $1.6 billion of NSF funding in the Giant Magellan Telescope (GMT) and the Thirty Meter Telescope (TMT), two gargantuan observatories in early phases of construction with an estimated total price tag in excess of $5 billion. With the GMT in the Southern Hemisphere–on a Chilean mountaintop–and the TMT in the Northern Hemisphere–either on the summit of Hawaii's Mauna Kea or a peak on La Palma in Spain's Canary Islands–U.S. astronomers would gain profound new views of the whole sky through these extremely powerful telescopic eyes.

Other than helping these twin titans across the finish line, the report also recommends that the NSF and DOE jointly spend $660 million to create the Cosmic Microwave Background Stage 4 Observatory (CMB-S4), a facility to survey the big bang's afterglow in exquisite detail. An additional $2.5 billion of NSF funds would go to building the Next-Generation Very Large Array (ngVLA), a radio observatory that would be 10 times more sensitive than the aging facilities it would replace. Additionally, Astro2020 strongly endorses further upgrades to two projects opening entirely novel windows on the cosmos: the Laser Interferometer Gravitational-Wave

Observatory (LIGO) and to the IceCube Neutrino Observatory, a facility with thousands of detectors arranged within a cubic kilometer of Antarctic ice. Paired with traditional observatories, LIGO and IceCube can help astronomers divine the arcane mechanics at play within the cores of exploding suns and between merging black holes and neutron stars.

Power to the People

The pathway forward may be clear, but abundant obstacles remain. Much depends on whether Congress and the White House fully embrace–and fund–Astro2020's recommendations, a not at all certain prospect in the modern era of hyperpolarized politics. Then there is the looming issue of satellite mega constellations. Despite their benefits for global broadband connectivity, these groups of satellites pose existential threats to multiple major projects via the optical and radio contamination they inescapably add to exquisitely delicate observations of the heavens. For that increasingly dire problem, Astro2020 offers only the rather dissatisfying solution of engaging in interagency, as well as international, collaboration to devise better, more protective regulatory frameworks.

But as the authors of the report themselves note, despite such challenges, the success of their audacious vision may ultimately hinge on how they handle the most valuable assets of U.S. astronomy, which are not dollars but people.

"Our report says serious attention also needs to be paid to investments in the foundations of this research–including in the people who carry it out," said Astro2020 steering committee co-chair Robert Kennicutt, an astronomer who holds professorships at the University of Arizona and Texas A&M University, in a statement.

That recognition, deep in the Decadal Survey's bones, is one reason Astro2020 is "a huge win for U.S. astronomy," says Scott Gaudi, an astronomer at the Ohio State University and co-chair of the HabEx mission concept study. "The decadal steering committee really thought about how to create a balanced portfolio–not just with a new set of Great Observatories and projects like the GMT and TMT but also with significant support for basic things like more research grants and mid-scale programs. And that's exactly what we need to make the more ambitious parts of this vision even plausible in the first place."

In recent years, the community has been left reeling not only from budget-blowing projects but also from sexual-harassment scandals, anemic support for early-career researchers and their smaller-scale projects, and brutal asymmetries in work-life balance that have led to burnout and poor well-being. There is also a worrisome lack of diversity among the ranks. In this melting-pot nation, the typical practitioners of astrophysics remain overwhelmingly white and male, with all the privileges, obvious or subtle, this entails–something keenly felt when, for instance, some of them seek to build new facilities on the sacred grounds of historically disenfranchised minority groups, as is the case of the TMT and the project's preferred construction site on Mauna Kea.

To remedy these and other social ills, Astro2020 recommends more spending on research grants and independent postdoctoral fellowships, increased funding and institutional support for diversity-boosting initiatives at the university and federal-agency level, and a formal recognition at NASA, the NSF, and the DOE that harassment and discrimination are corrosive forms of scientific misconduct. With the TMT imbroglio at Mauna Kea clearly in mind, the report also calls for a "community astronomy" model of engagement that would seek to "respect, empower, and benefit local communities while advancing scientific research," according to a National Academies press release.

Such acts, says University of New Hampshire cosmologist Chanda Prescod-Weinstein, would be "steps in the right direction" to address the growing storm of cultural crisis cresting over the field's horizons. But even so–especially in the case of engaging with historically marginalized indigenous people–she says this Decadal Survey's recommendations do not go far enough.

"Sometimes scientists have to accept a hard 'no' from indigenous people," Prescod-Weinstein says. "Instead [Astro2020] focuses more on what the characteristics and quality of a collaboration between indigenous communities and scientists should be. It never directly acknowledges the scenario that indigenous people may not want to collaborate.... My view may change once I've had more time to sit with the report, but my first impression is that scientific goals are still supreme and that we are still not ready, as a community, to talk to nonastronomer indigenous people as if they are our equals and their concerns matter as much as ours."

About the Author

Lee Billings is a senior editor for space and physics at Scientific American.

How to Search for Life as We Don't Know It

By Avi Loeb

In my freshman seminar at Harvard last semester, I mentioned that the nearest star to the sun, Proxima Centauri, emits mostly infrared radiation and has a planet, Proxima b, in the habitable zone around it. As a challenge to the students, I asked: "Suppose there are creatures crawling on the surface of Proxima b? What would their infrared-sensitive eyes look like?" The brightest student in class responded within seconds with an image of the mantis shrimp, which possesses infrared vision. The shrimp's eyes look like two ping-pong balls connected with cords to its head. "It looks like an alien," she whispered.

When trying to imagine something we've never seen, we often default to something we have seen. For that reason, in our search for extraterrestrial life we are usually looking for life as we know it. But is there a path for expanding our imagination to life as we don't know it?

In physics, an analogous path was already established a century ago and turned out to be successful in many contexts. It involves conducting laboratory experiments that reveal the underlying laws of physics, which in turn apply to the entire universe. For example, around the same time when the neutron was discovered in the laboratory of James Chadwick in 1932, Lev Landau suggested that there might be stars made of neutrons. Astronomers realized subsequently that there are, in fact, some 100 million neutron stars in our Milky Way galaxy alone–and a billion times more in the observable universe. Recently, the LIGO experiment detected gravitational-wave signals from collisions between neutron stars at cosmological distances. It is now thought that such collisions produce the precious gold that is forged into wedding bands. The moral of this story is that physicists were able to imagine something new in the universe at large and search for it in the sky by following insights gained from laboratory experiments on Earth.

The search for extraterrestrial life can follow a similar approach. By creating synthetic life in various ways from a soup of chemicals in the lab, we might be able to imagine new environments where life might occur differently than on Earth. The situation is similar to composing a recipe book with prescriptions for baking different types of cakes. In order to write a rich recipe book, we need to experiment with many types of chemicals. And also, as I noted in a paper with Manasvi Lingam, this experimentation may use fluids other than water, which is considered essential for life as we know it.

One of my Harvard colleagues, the Nobel laureate Jack Szostak, is getting close to creating synthetic life in his laboratory. Any success with a single recipe may suggest variations that would produce a diversity of outcomes, to be assembled into our recipe book for synthetic life. By identifying suitable environmental conditions from our laboratory experiments, we can later search for real systems where they are realized in the sky, just as in the case of neutron stars.

In following this approach, we should be as careful as we are in tapping nuclear energy. Creating artificial variants of life in our laboratories brings the risk of causing an environmental disaster, as imagined in the story of Frankenstein. Such experimentation must be performed in isolated environments so that mishaps with life as we don't know it will not endanger the life we know.

Although the surfaces of planets and asteroids can be explored remotely for biological signatures, extraterrestrial life might be most abundant under the surface. Habitable conditions could exist in the oceans that lie under thick icy surfaces, not only within moons like Saturn's Enceladus or Jupiter's Europa, but also inside free-floating objects in interstellar space. In other research with Lingam, we showed that the number of life-bearing objects could exceed the number of rocky planets in the habitable zone around stars by many orders of magnitude.

The adaptation of life to extreme environments could take exotic forms, as exemplified by extremophiles on Earth. For example, frozen microscopic animals were recently discovered to survive 24,000 years in the Siberian permafrost, and microbial life was found to persist 100 million years beneath the seafloor. These microbes were born during the warm Cretaceous period when dinosaurs dominated Earth.

In the solar system, the closest conditions to Earth were realized on its nearest neighbors, Venus and Mars. NASA recently selected two new missions to study Venus, and its Perseverance rover is searching for traces of life on Mars. If extraterrestrial life is found, the key follow-up question is whether it is "life as we know it." If not, we will realize that there are multiple chemical pathways to natural life. But if we find evidence for Martian or Venusian life that resembles terrestrial life, then this might indicate a special preference for "life as we know it." Alternatively, life could have been transported by rocks that traveled between planets through a process called panspermia. My student Amir Siraj and I wrote a paper showing that the transfer of life could have been mediated by planet-grazing asteroids. We should also keep in mind the very remote possibility that life was seeded in the inner solar system by an "extrasolar gardener," namely through "directed panspermia".

My most vivid childhood memory is of dinner conversations in which the adults in the room pretended to know much more than they actually did. This was undoubtedly a form of "intellectual makeup" that they wore to improve their appearance. And if I asked a question to which these pretenders had no ready answer, they would dismiss it as irrelevant. My experience as a senior scientist is no different, especially when asking the question: "Are we the smartest kid on the cosmic block?"

Science offers the privilege of maintaining our childhood curiosity. The advance of scientific knowledge through experimentation cannot be stopped. Here's hoping that we will find a recipe for artificial life that will allow us to imagine something far more intelligent than the natural life we encountered so far. This will be a humbling experience. But even if we will not discover this supreme intelligence in our laboratories, its by-products may just show up in our sky as mail posted from faraway neighborhoods in the Milky Way. And we'll be searching for that through the telescopes of the recently announced Galileo Project.

This is an opinion and analysis article; the views expressed by the author or authors are not necessarily those of Scientific American.

About the Author

Avi Loeb is former chair (2011-2020) of the astronomy department at Harvard University, founding director of Harvard's Black Hole Initiative and director of the Institute for Theory and Computation at the Harvard-Smithsonian Center for Astrophysics. He also chairs the Board on Physics and Astronomy of the National Academies and the advisory board for the Breakthrough Starshot project, and is a member of President's Council of Advisors on Science and Technology. Loeb is the bestselling author of Extraterrestrial: The First Sign of Intelligent Life Beyond Earth *(Houghton Mifflin Harcourt).*

Section 3: Are We Alone?

Alone in a Crowded Milky Way

By Caleb A. Scharf

On January 15, 1790, nine mutineers from HMS *Bounty*, 18 people from Tahiti, and one baby arrived on Pitcairn Island—one of the most isolated habitable places on the planet. Surrounded by the southern Pacific Ocean and with hundreds of miles of open water between it and the nearest other islands, Pitcairn is the epitome of solitude.

Before the *Bounty* escapees showed up, the island may not have seen human occupation of any kind since the 1400s, when it was still inhabited by Polynesians. That community perhaps existed for centuries—centuries that seem to have culminated with a depletion of natural resources, as well as conflicts on other, distant islands that cut off lines of trade and supply, leading to the effective extinction of Pitcairn's human occupants. What was, at least superficially, a habitable place had become unsustainable, until the arrival of the *Bounty* on that fateful day in 1790. Remarkably, it took another 18 years for any other ship to drop anchor at Pitcairn, even though the settlers recorded sightings of vessels passing in the distance.

The story of Pitcairn is just one extreme example of the unusual dynamics of human occupation across the southern Pacific. Within the regions of Polynesia, Micronesia, and Melanesia, there are tens of thousands of islands scattered across millions of square miles of ocean. Many are barely more than a protuberance of rock and coral, and even the habitable spots are not all inhabited at any given time. But taken together, they represent a vast landscape of potential settlement and civilization for people motivated to navigate across Earth's watery depths.

The parallels between this unmistakably terrestrial environment and our cosmic surroundings are striking. In the Milky Way galaxy, there are perhaps as many as 300 billion stars. The best estimates from exoplanet-hunting efforts, such as those undertaken with

NASA's Kepler space telescope, suggest that within this ocean of stellar bodies there may be more than 10 billion small, rocky worlds in orbital configurations conducive to temperate surface conditions. Like the islands of Earth, these exoplanetary specks might both generate and support living systems and could provide a network of waypoints for any species determined to migrate across interstellar space. And that is where things get really interesting.

Just as Western Europeans eventually realized that the peoples of the southern Pacific had spread across its thousands of miles of ocean on simple vessels gliding along at just a few knots, we can now see that spreading across our galaxy need not require much more than persistence and a modest amount of cosmic time.

Most famously, over a lunch in 1950 with fellow scientists, physicist Enrico Fermi first recognized this fact and–as the story goes–blurted out, "Don't you ever wonder where everybody is?" The "everybody" in this case was any spacefaring species, and the question developed over time into the equally famous, albeit somewhat mislabeled, Fermi paradox: unless technologically proficient species are vanishingly rare, they should have spread practically everywhere across the galaxy by now, yet we see no evidence for them. Fermi, renowned for his ability to carry out so-called back-of-the-envelope calculations in his head, had figured out in approximate terms that the Milky Way could be settled in the blink of a cosmic eye when each tick of the galactic clock accounts for millions of years.

In 1975 astrophysicist Michael Hart produced the first properly quantitative and nuanced study of this idea, in which he put forward what has become known as Hart's "fact A." This refers to the absence of aliens on Earth today. That unassailable fact (for most level-headed people) led Hart to the conclusion that no other technological civilizations currently exist–or have ever existed–in our galaxy. The key to this assertion, much as with Fermi's original insight, lies in the relatively short amount of time it would apparently take for a species to spread across the Milky Way's 100,000-light-year girth even using modest, far-slower-than-light propulsion systems.

Physicist Frank Tipler also studied the problem, and he reported on his work in 1980, demonstrating, much like Hart, that in a few million years suitably motivated aliens could indeed visit everywhere. Given that our solar system has been around for 4.5 billion years and that the Milky Way assembled at least 10 billion years ago, there has been more than enough time for species to wind up on all inhabitable worlds.

Critically, though, these investigations considered the spread of life somewhat differently. Hart assumed a process of settlement "in the flesh" by a biological species, whereas Tipler imagined star-hopping swarms of self-replicating machine probes that would spread without restraint. In most settlement scenarios, the stellar systems and their planets become inhabited, if they were not already, and then serve as the next base of operations for launching onward to new systems. For Tipler's self-replicating machines, the primary limits to their expansion would be the availability of sufficient energy and raw materials for making each subsequent generation.

These radically different approaches highlight the challenges of making meaningful statements about interstellar migration. There are always a lot of big assumptions in any study like these. Some are reasonable and easily justifiable, but others are trickier. For example, all scenarios involve guesses about the scope of the technology used for interstellar travel. Furthermore, when the species is "along for the ride" rather than sending out sophisticated robotic emissaries, the most fundamental assumption is that living things can survive any kind of interstellar travel at all.

We know that traveling at even a paltry 10 percent of the speed of light requires some pretty wild technology—for example, fusion-bomb propulsion or colossal laser-driven light sails. There also has to be shielding from the hull-eroding impacts of interstellar gas atoms, as well as from starship-destroying crumbs of rock, each of which carries the punch of a bomb for a spacecraft at any decent fraction of light speed. Traveling at more modest speeds is potentially much safer but results in transit times between stars of centuries or millennia—and it is far from obvious how to keep a crew alive and well for time spans that may greatly exceed individual lifetimes.

Elsewhere in the galaxy there may be archipelagos of interstellar species for whom cosmic visitors are the norm.

The most contentious assumptions, though, revolve around questions of motivation and the projections we make about the longevity of entire civilizations and their settlements. For example, if an alien species is simply not interested in reaching other stars, the whole idea of galactic settlement literally stalls. This was one argument put forward by Carl Sagan and William Newman in 1983 as a rebuttal to what they called the "solipsist approach" to extraterrestrial intelligence. But as my colleague astronomer Jason Wright points out, this kind of proposition is itself arguably a "monocultural fallacy." To put this another way: it seems impossible to speculate with any accuracy about the behavior of an entire species as if it were thinking with one unified mind. We humans certainly do not fit in that box. And even if the vast majority of the Milky Way's putative spacefaring civilizations do not attempt galactic diasporas, all it may take is one culture going against the grain to spread signs of life and technology across hundreds of billions of star systems.

In fact, the history of Fermi's paradox is awash with diverse debates on its underlying suppositions, as well as with a huge variety of posited "solutions." Few, if any, of these solutions are readily testable. Although some include ideas that are pretty straightforward, others are strictly science fiction. For example, it could be that the cost in resources of attaining the ability to rapidly traverse interstellar space is too high even for a superbly technological species. That could certainly trim the number of explorers and explain Hart's fact A. Or perhaps population growth is not, as many researchers have supposed, a strong motivation for voyaging to the stars, especially for a species that restrains any rapacious impulses and develops a truly sustainable existence in its home system. The ultimate green revolution would remove the impetus to go farther afield for anything other than scientific exploration.

Sounding a more ominous note are concepts such as the "great filter"–the idea that there is something that always limits a species, perhaps an inevitable failure to achieve that green revolution, leading to an implosive extinction of all potentially technological life. Alternatively, maybe natural cataclysms, from supernovae explosions to outbursts from the Milky Way's central black hole, simply prune galactic life regularly enough to keep it from becoming widespread.

More outrageous proposals include the zoo hypothesis. In this scenario, we are being kept deliberately isolated and in the dark by alien powers that be. There is also what I like to call the paranoia scenario: other civilizations are out there but are hiding from one another and refusing to communicate because of some kind of cosmic xenophobia.

Perhaps, though, there are simpler ways to explain our current ignorance about aliens. Those answers could share characteristics with the example right under our noses–the time-varying and patchy nature of human occupation in the islands of the South Pacific. In both terrestrial and extraterrestrial cases, there are basic, universal factors at play, from the scarcity of good places to drop anchor to the time it might take for a population to ready itself to push farther across the void.

Back in 2015 my colleague Adam Frank of the University of Rochester and I were having lunch near Columbia University's campus in New York City. As at Fermi's lunch 65 years earlier, the conversation was about the nature of spacefaring species. And inspired by Fermi's spur-of-the-moment mental calculation, we were trying to craft an investigative strategy that made the fewest possible unsubstantiated assumptions and that could be somehow tested or constrained with real data. At the center of this exercise was the simple thought that, just as with Pitcairn Island's transitory occupants, waves of exploration or settlement could come and go across the galaxy, with humans happening to emerge in one of the lonely periods.

This idea relates to Hart's original fact A: that there is no evidence here on Earth today of extraterrestrial explorers. But it goes further by asking whether we can obtain meaningful limits on galactic life by constraining the exact length of time over which Earth might have gone unvisited. Perhaps long, long ago aliens came and went. A number of scientists have, over the years, discussed the possibility of looking for artifacts that might have been left behind after such visitations of our solar system. The necessary scope of a complete search is hard to predict, but the situation on Earth alone turns out to be a bit more manageable. In 2018 another of my colleagues, Gavin Schmidt of NASA's Goddard Institute for Space Studies, together with Adam Frank, produced a critical assessment of whether we could even tell if there had been an earlier industrial civilization on our planet.

As fantastic as it may seem, Schmidt and Frank argue–as do most planetary scientists–that it is actually very easy for time to erase essentially all signs of technological life on Earth. The only real evidence after a million or more years would boil down to isotopic or chemical stratigraphic anomalies–odd features such as synthetic molecules, plastics, or radioactive fallout. Fossil remains and other paleontological markers are so rare and so contingent on special conditions of formation that they might not tell us anything in this case.

Indeed, modern human urbanization covers only on order of about 1 percent of the planetary surface, providing a very small target area for any paleontologists in the distant future. Schmidt and Frank also conclude that nobody has yet performed the necessary experiments to look exhaustively for such nonnatural signatures on Earth. The bottom line is, if an industrial civilization on the scale of our own had existed a few million years ago, we might not know about it. That absolutely does not mean one existed; it indicates only that the possibility cannot be rigorously eliminated.

Over the past few years we have pursued the grander, galaxy-wide implications of these ideas in an investigation led by Jonathan Carroll-Nellenback of the University of Rochester and with Jason Wright of the Pennsylvania State University. A key advance has been the development of a series of agent-based computer simulations, backed up by old-fashioned paper-and-pencil mathematics, enabling us to build a more realistic picture of how species might move around in a galaxy that is itself full of motion.

If you take a snapshot of stars within a couple of hundred light-years of the sun, you will find that they are moving like the particles in a gas. Relative to any fixed point in this space, a star may be moving rapidly or slowly and in what is effectively a random direction. Zoom out farther, to scales of thousands of light-years, and you will begin to register the grand, shared orbital motion that carries a star such as our sun around the Milky Way once every 230 million years or so. Stars much closer to the galactic center take much less time to complete a circuit, and there are fast-moving "halo" stars diving in and out of the plane of the galactic disk as part of a distinct, rather spherically shaped swarm surrounding that disk.

What this means is that for a civilization looking around itself for target stars to explore, what is closest and what will be closest in the future vary significantly over time. A good illustration of this is our own solar system. Right now our nearest star, Proxima Centauri, is 4.24 light-years away, but in about 10,000 years it will be only 3.5 light-years distant–a significant savings in interstellar travel time. If we were to wait until about 37,000 years from today, our nearest neighbor would for a time be a small red dwarf star called Ross 248, which would then be a mere three light-years from us.

To model this shifting stellar map, our simulation uses a three-dimensional box of stars, with movements akin to those in a small part of a real galaxy. It then initiates a "front" of settlement by assigning a selection of those stars as hosts to spacefaring civilizations. Those civilizations have finite life spans, so a system can also become unoccupied. And a civilization has a waiting period before it is capable of launching a probe or settlement effort to its nearest neighboring star. All these factors can be altered, tweaked and explored to see how they affect the outcome. For a wide range of possibilities, a somewhat raggedy-looking settlement front self-propagates through interstellar space. The speed of this propagating front is the key to cross-checking and confirming possible solutions to Fermi's original puzzle.

What we find is both simple and subtle. First, the natural, gaslike motion of stars in the galaxy means that even the slowest interstellar probes, moving at some 30 kilometers per second (nearly twice as fast as *Voyager 1*'s current speed of 17 kilometers per second in its outbound motion from our sun), would ensure that a settlement front would cross the galaxy in much less than a billion years. If we factor in other stellar motions, from galactic rotation or halo stars, this time span only shrinks. In other words, just as Fermi saw, it is not hard to fill the galaxy with life. But it is also the case that exactly how "filled" the galaxy becomes depends on both the number of genuinely settleable worlds out there–what we have dubbed the Aurora effect in homage to Kim Stanley Robinson's epic 2015 science-fiction novel *Aurora*–and the length of the period civilizations are able to endure on a world.

At one extreme, it is easy to make the galaxy empty by simply shrinking the number of usable planets and having civilizations last for only, say, 100,000 years or so. At the other extreme, it is easy to tweak these factors to fill space with active spacefaring settlements. In fact, if suitable worlds are numerous enough, it almost does not matter how long settled civilizations last on average. If they retain the technology that allowed them to travel in the first place, then enough of them could carry on exploring and eventually fill the galaxy.

But it is between these extremes that the most compelling and potentially realistic situations arise. When the frequency of occurrence of settleable worlds in a galaxy is intermediate between high and very low, fascinating things can happen. Specifically, ordinary statistical fluctuations in the number and location of suitable worlds in patches of galactic space can create clusters of systems that are continually visited or resettled by wave after wave of interstellar explorers. Think of it as an archipelago, a group or chain of islands. The flip side to the existence of these clusters is that they are typically surrounded by large unsettled regions of space, places just too far and too sparsely distributed to bother setting out for.

Can this "galactic archipelago" scenario explain our situation on Earth? Remarkably, it may. For example, if typical planetary civilizations can last for a million years and if only 3 percent of star systems are actually settleable, there is a roughly 10 percent probability that a planet like Earth has not been visited in at least the past million years. In other words, it is not terribly unlikely that we would find ourselves on the lonely side of the equation.

Conversely, this scenario implies that elsewhere in the galaxy there are clusters, archipelagos, of interstellar species for whom cosmic neighbors or visitors are the norm. No extreme hypotheses are needed for any of this to take place; it would require just a rather ordinary accounting of planetary numbers and the nature of stellar movements amid the swirling stars of the Milky Way. And although it is true that assumptions linger about the feasibility of any kind of interstellar travel and about the likelihood that a species will actually undertake it, other factors are just parameters to be tuned. Some, such as the number of inhabitable worlds, are in astronomers' sights already as we seek greater knowledge of exoplanets. Others, such as the longevity of civilizations, are the subject of intense scrutiny as we attempt to deal with our own issues of planetary sustainability.

The possibility also exists for us to discover evidence of settled stellar archipelagos or the ongoing propagation of a settlement front. Targeting our searches for extraterrestrial intelligence and technology not on individual, known exoplanets but rather on galactic regions where the topography of stars might lend itself to interstellar expansion or clustering could be an interesting new strategy. Until recently, our three-dimensional map of galactic space was woefully limited, but with instruments such as the European Space Agency's Gaia observatory mapping a billion astronomical objects and stellar motions, we might be able to chart these hotspots.

In the end, though, the true paradox of Fermi's paradox may be that there is no paradox at all. What my colleagues' work shows is that it is an entirely natural state for a habitable, inhabited world such as Earth to exhibit no discernible evidence of having ever been visited or settled by an extraterrestrial species. This is true whether the galaxy is devoid of other technologically advanced life or is as teeming as it can be with interstellar explorers. Just as Pitcairn may have sat unoccupied for as much as three centuries in the Pacific Ocean, Earth might simply be passing through a period of isolation before the cosmic ripple of pan-galactic life washes over it once again.

The real question, as it was for Polynesian settlers across the centuries, is whether our planetary civilization will still be here when that happens.

About the Author

Caleb Scharf is director of the Columbia Astrobiology Center and author of several books, including The Copernicus Complex *(2014) and* The Zoomable Universe *(2017). He writes the* Life, Unbounded *blog for* Scientific American *and has written for many other publications. He lives in New York City with his wife and two daughters.*

If There Are Aliens Out There, Where Are They?

By Mario Livio, Joe Silk

Physicist Enrico Fermi famously asked the question "Where are they?" to express his surprise over the absence of any signs for the existence of other intelligent civilizations in the Milky Way galaxy. Although many potential resolutions to this so-called Fermi paradox have been suggested over the years, there is still no consensus on which one, if any, is correct. The question of whether we are alone in the Milky Way (or in the universe at large) remains, however, one of the most intriguing questions in science in general and in astronomy in particular.

Given the enormous uncertainties involved with the emergence, evolution, and survivability of any extrasolar life (if it exists), we shall attempt to briefly identify the most generic, remotely detectable signatures of alien life (both simple and intelligent) and to examine the expected effectiveness of various search strategies. This topic has become particularly timely, because observations (primarily with the Kepler space telescope) have shown that the Milky Way contains no fewer than a billion Earth-size planets orbiting sun-like (or smaller) stars in the Goldilocks region that allows for liquid water to exist on the planet's surface (the so-called habitable zone). Furthermore, the search for extraterrestrial intelligent life has recently received a significant boost in the form of "Breakthrough Listen"—a $100-million decade-long project aimed at searching for non-natural transmissions in the electromagnetic bandwidth from 100 megahertz to 50 gigahertz.

Simple life appeared on Earth almost as soon as the planet cooled sufficiently to support water-based organisms. To be detectable from a distance, however, life has to evolve to the point where it dominates the planetary surface chemistry and has significantly changed the atmosphere, creating chemical "biosignatures" that can in principle be detected remotely. For instance, Earth itself would probably not have been detected as a life-bearing planet during the first 2 billion years of its existence. Concerning the evolution of intelligent life, the main open questions include:

–What are the geochemical constraints on the evolution of complex life?

–What are the timescales that those constraints dictate?

–Are there evolutionary "filters" or bottlenecks that make it extremely hard to make the transition to intelligence? On Earth, for example, it took about 3 billion years for the most basic multi-cellular life forms to appear. It took 4 1/2 billion years (and a series of contingencies such as plate tectonics and asteroid impacts) to reach even the most rudimentary capability of interstellar communication. (That is, via radio reception and transmission.) These considerations demonstrate that it is important to first establish whether planetary systems that are older than the solar system are common in the Milky Way.

The current age of the solar system is about half that of the our galaxy's disk and also half of the sun's predicted lifetime. We therefore expect that roughly one half of the stars in our galactic disk are older than the sun. A recent study that examined planet formation history concluded that the solar system formed close to the median epoch for giant planet formation, and that about 80 percent of currently existing Earth-like planets may already had been formed at the time of Earth's formation. This gives us great leverage for probing extrasolar intelligent life.

Which detectable biosignature may be considered the most reliable for the existence of simple life (on a sufficiently old, rocky planet, in the habitable zone)? Even though no single biosignature would be absolutely compelling, an atmosphere that is very rich in oxygen (say 20 percent or more) would probably be the most promising target initially. Wheras nonbiological processes (such as the splitting of carbon dioxide by intense ultraviolet radiation) can produce oxygen in a planetary atmosphere, only under rare circumstances would these create such high levels of enrichment.

Only in combination with other potential biosignatures, however, such as methane, would the credibility of a life-based origin for the oxygen be significantly strengthened.

Consequently, an excellent first step in the quest for signatures of simple extrasolar life in the relatively near future would be to: search for oxygen, but try to back it up with other biosignatures. This can (in principle) be achieved with large, ground-based arrays of relatively low-cost flux collector telescopes (such as a next-generation European Extremely Large Telescope; with a collecting area the size of a few football fields), if these are equipped with very-high-dispersion spectrographs. The oxygen lines from the exoplanet's spectrum would be slightly Doppler-shifted relative to oxygen in Earth's atmosphere, making it relatively straightforward (although definitely not easy) to detect them. The more difficult detection of methane in the infrared would have to follow.

What would be the requirements from a space mission? We would want to be able to at least place a meaningful constraint on the rarity of extrasolar life, if such a mission happens to not detect any biosignatures. Simulations show that in the case of nondetection, to be able to make a statement such as: "remotely detectable life occurs in less than about 10 percent of Earth-like planets around sun-like stars," would require the ability to image and characterize the atmospheres of at least three dozen or so exoEarths. Such a yield, in turn, would necessitate a space telescope aperture exceeding about 8.5 meters in diameter. The proposed Habitable-Exoplanet Imaging Mission (HabEx), under discussion for the next decadal survey, would have to be designed at the upper limit of its currently conceived aperture to meet this particular requirement. The more ambitious nine- to 12-meter Large UV/Optical/IR (LUVOIR) type space telescope such as the proposed high-definition space telescope would be a natural mission candidate for the 2030s.

One would ideally like to go beyond biosignatures and seek the clearest sign of an alien technological civilization. This could be the unambiguous detection of an intelligent, non-natural signal, most notably via radio transmission, the aim of the SETI (Search for Extraterrestrial Intelligence) program. Yet there is a distinct possibility that radio communication might be considered archaic to an advanced life form. Its use might have been short-lived in most civilizations and hence rare over large volumes of the universe. What might then be a generic signature? Energy consumption is a hallmark of an advanced civilization that appears to be virtually impossible to conceal.

The two most plausible, long-term energy sources available to an advanced technology are through commanding stellar luminosity with a construction known as a "Dyson sphere," possibly including harvesting the starlight from many stars, not just one or even from an entire galaxy; the other is by controlled fusion of hydrogen into heavier nuclei. In both cases, waste heat would be an inevitable outcome, producing a detectable mid-infrared (MIR) signature. Other potential signatures of advanced civilizations that have also been suggested, such as various forms of atmospheric industrial pollution, or short-lived radioactive products, are necessarily transitory. (Basically those aliens either clean up their act or destroy themselves). Infrared emission, on the other hand, seems almost unavoidable. A recent large survey by the Wide-field Infrared Survey Explorer (WISE) satellite did identify five red spiral galaxies whose combination of high MIR and low near-ultraviolet luminosities are inconsistent with simple expectations from high rates of star formation. A conventional explanation for these observations, such as the presence of large amounts of internal dust, has not been ruled out, however. Such peculiar objects deserve follow-up observations before we explore whether they might represent the signatures of galaxy-dominating species.

More pessimistically, biologically based intelligence may constitute only a very brief phase in the evolution of complexity, followed by what futurists have dubbed the "singularity"–the dominance of artificial, inorganic intelligence. If this is indeed the case, most advanced species are likely not to be found on a planet's surface (where gravity is helpful for the emergence of biological life, but is otherwise a liability). But they probably must still be near a fuel supply, namely a star, because of energy considerations. Even if such intelligent machines were to transmit a signal, it would probably be unrecognizable and nondecodable to our relatively primitive organic brains.

This could perhaps explain the Fermi paradox. If this scenario holds true, our chances of detecting simple life via biosignatures may be far greater than those of discovering intelligent ET's. Still, the ultimate goal of detecting the signature of an advanced intelligence, whether biological or nonbiological, remains the most intriguing option. All power to proposed projects for the 2020s such as Japan's Space Infrared Telescope for Cosmology and Astrophysics (SPICA) and NASA's Far Infrared Surveyor.

The key point is that for the first time in human history, we are only two or three decades away from being able to actually answer the "Are we alone?" question. Because the answer may affect nothing less than our last claim for being special in the cosmos, its importance cannot be overemphasized. In any case, echoing what Giuseppe Cocconi and Philip Morrison said at the end of their seminal 1960 *Nature* article on searching for extraterrestrials, we shall never know unless we search! (*Scientific American* is part of Nature Publishing Group.)

This article is based on research conducted at the Institut d'Astrophysique de Paris.

About the Authors

Mario Livio is an astrophysicist and author. His most recent book is Galileo: And the Science Deniers.

Joseph Silk is Homewood Professor of Physics and Astronomy at the Johns Hopkins University in Baltimore and a researcher at Institut d'Astrophysique de Paris and Service d'Astrophysique, CEASaclay in France. He has published more than 700 articles and several popular books.

Alien Hunters Discover Mysterious Signal from Proxima Centauri

By Jonathan O'Callaghan, Lee Billings

It's never aliens—until it is. On December 18, news leaked in the British newspaper the *Guardian* of a mysterious signal coming from the closest star to our own, Proxima Centauri, a star too dim to see from Earth with the naked eye that is nonetheless a cosmic stone's throw away at just 4.2 light-years. Found this autumn in archival data gathered last year, the signal appears to emanate from the direction of our neighboring star and cannot yet be dismissed as Earth-based interference, raising the very faint prospect that it is a transmission from some form of advanced extraterrestrial intelligence (ETI)—a so-called technosignature. Now, speaking to *Scientific American*, the scientists behind the discovery caution there is still much work to be done, but admit the interest is justified. "It has some particular properties that caused it to pass many of our checks, and we cannot yet explain it," says Andrew Siemion from the University of California, Berkeley.

Most curiously, it occupies a very narrow band of the radio spectrum: 982 megahertz, specifically, which is a region typically bereft of transmissions from human-made satellites and spacecraft. "We don't know of any natural way to compress electromagnetic energy into a single bin in frequency" such as this one, Siemion says. Perhaps, he says, some as-yet-unknown exotic quirk of plasma physics could be a natural explanation for the tantalizingly concentrated radio waves. But "for the moment, the only source that we know of is technological."

The detection was made by a $100 million project called Breakthrough Listen, led by Siemion and funded by tech billionaire Yuri Milner under the umbrella of Milner's Breakthrough Initiatives. The goal of this multiyear endeavor—which began in 2015 with a star-studded announcement attended by Stephen Hawking and other space-science luminaries–is to buy observing time on radio telescopes around the world to search the skies for evidence of technological civilizations. That pursuit, of course, is more commonly known as the Search for Extraterrestrial Intelligence (SETI). To date, no such evidence has conclusively been found despite more than a half century of modest-but-steady SETI activity, with any potential signals almost always ruled out as originating from satellites orbiting Earth or other human-caused interference.

"If you see such a signal and it's not coming from the surface of Earth, you know you have detected extraterrestrial technology," says Jason Wright, a SETI-centric astronomer at Penn State University in Pennsylvania. "Unfortunately, humans have launched a lot of extraterrestrial technology."

The story of this latest SETI spectacle really began April 29, 2019, when scientists affiliated with Breakthrough Listen started collecting the data that would later reveal the intriguing signal. A team had been using the Parkes radio telescope in Australia to study Proxima Centauri for signs of flares coming from the red dwarf star, in part to understand how such flares might affect Proxima's planets. The system hosts at least two worlds. The first, dubbed Proxima b upon its discovery in 2016, is about 1.2 times the size of Earth and in an 11-day orbit. Proxima b resides in the star's "habitable zone," a hazily defined sector in which liquid water could exist upon a rocky planet's surface–provided, that is, Proxima Centauri's intense stellar flares have not sputtered away a world's atmosphere. Another planet, the roughly seven-Earth-mass Proxima c, was discovered in 2019 in a frigid 5.2-year orbit.

Using Parkes, the astronomers had observed the star for 26 hours as part of their stellar-flare study, but, as is routine within the Breakthrough Listen project, they also flagged the resulting data for a later look to seek out any candidate SETI signals. The task fell to a young intern in Siemion's SETI program at Berkeley, Shane Smith, who is also an undergraduate student at Hillsdale College. Smith began sifting through the data in June of this year, but it was not until late October that he stumbled upon the curious narrowband emission, needle-sharp at 982.002 megahertz, hidden in plain view in the Proxima Centauri observations. From there, things happened fast–with good reason. "It's the most exciting signal that we've found in the Breakthrough Listen project, because we haven't had a signal jump through this many of our filters before," says Sofia Sheikh from Penn State University, who helmed the subsequent analysis of the signal for Breakthrough Listen and is the lead author on an upcoming paper detailing that work, which will be published in early 2021. Soon, the team began calling the signal by a more formal name: BLC1, for "Breakthrough Listen Candidate 1."

To pique any SETI researcher's interest, a signal must first endure a barrage of simple automated tests to rule out obvious terrestrial interference. Hundreds of candidates, however, routinely pass this phase and are singled out for further investigation. From there, almost all will be dismissed as some mirage or error–perhaps an excess of static, for instance–that fooled the winnowing algorithm, eliminating them from consideration as any sort of transmission from talkative aliens. "Except this one," Sheikh says.

Revisiting the data from 2019, Sheikh and her colleagues noted that the telescope had looked at Proxima multiple times in scans lasting 30 minutes over the course of a week. Breakthrough Listen uses a technique called "nodding," where the telescope will spend a period of time looking at a target and then an equivalent period looking elsewhere in the sky, to check that any potential signal is truly coming from the target and not, say, someone microwaving their lunch in an observatory's cafeteria. "In five of the 30-minute observations over about three hours we see this thing come back," Sheikh says, a hint that the signal indeed originated from Proxima Centauri–or some other deep-space source in that part of the sky–before making its way to Earth.

One might think, then, that the case would be closed. But while a natural cosmic source may seem unlikely, it cannot yet be ruled out–and, the thinking goes, as unlikely as a natural explanation might be, an "unnatural" explanation such as aliens is even less likely still. Consequently, every member of the Breakthrough Listen team interviewed for this article steadfastly insists the chance of this being anything other than terrestrial interference is exceedingly remote. "The most likely thing is that it's some human cause," says Pete Worden, executive director of the Breakthrough Initiatives. "And when I say most likely, it's like 99.9 [percent]."

That rational skepticism extends all the way to the top. "When we launched Breakthrough Listen with Stephen Hawking in 2015," Milner says, "it was understood that the most rigorous scientific approach will be used to analyze all candidate signals." Milner and seemingly all the SETI researchers his funding supports fully expect BLC1 to wither away under the project's now-intense scrutiny. But, just maybe, it won't.

For the time being, months of further analysis are in store to definitively rule out other potential sources. And BLC1 itself, while seeming to come from Proxima Centauri, does not quite fit expectations for a technosignature from that system. First, the signal bears no trace of modulation–tweaks to its properties that can be used to convey information. "BLC1 is, for all intents and purposes, just a tone, just one note," Siemion says. "It has absolutely no additional features that we can discern at this point." And second, the signal "drifts," meaning that it appears to be changing very slightly in frequency–an effect that could be due to the motion of our planet, or of a moving extraterrestrial source such as a transmitter on the surface of one of Proxima Centauri's worlds. But the drift is the reverse of what one would naively expect for a signal originating from a world twirling around our sun's nearest neighboring star. "We would expect the signal to be going down in frequency like a trombone," Sheikh says. "What we see instead is like a slide whistle–the frequency goes up."

So far, follow-up observations using Parkes have failed to turn up the signal again, with a repeat observation being a necessity to confirm that BLC1 is a genuine technosignature. "If it's an ETI it must eventually be replicable, because it's unlikely it would be a one-off," says Shami Chatterjee, a radio astronomer from Cornell University in New York. "If an independent team at an independent observatory can recover the same signal, then hell yes. I would bet money that they won't, but I would love to be wrong."

Nonetheless, it remains one of the most intriguing signals found by Breakthrough Listen—or indeed any SETI program—to date, one that Sheikh compares to the so-called "Wow! signal" detected in 1977, which some believed to be of extraterrestrial origin. "I think it's on par with the Wow! signal," she says. More likely than not, however, this is simply some previously unknown source of Earth-based interference. In a few months we'll likely know for certain one way or another. But for the time being, it's never aliens—right? "I hate that phrase, because if you say that, then why even look?" Wright says. "What we mean by that is that it's never been aliens before."

About the Authors

Jonathan O'Callaghan is a freelance journalist covering commercial spaceflight, space exploration and astrophysics.

Lee Billings is a senior editor for space and physics at Scientific American.

Aliens Might Already Be Watching Us

By Tess Joosse

On June 25, the Pentagon and the Office of the Director of National Intelligence released their much hyped report on unidentified aerial phenomena, or UAP. Space alien enthusiasts and skeptics alike awaited it with bated breath. And while the report did not rule out an extraterrestrial origin for much of the documented UAP, it was short on details or bombshells.

But we already know our world is easily detectable by extrasolar observers. A paper published on June 23 in *Nature* shows that in the past 5,000 years, 1,715 stars have been in the right celestial position to view a populated Earth transiting the sun–with 319 more entering this sweet spot in the next 5,000 years. And seven of these far-off stars are known to have their own orbiting exoplanets that might support life.

"Instead of constantly saying, 'What can we detect from other worlds?' and 'Where are the other worlds that we can detect?' think about it the other way," says Jackie Faherty, an astronomer at the American Museum of Natural History in New York City and a co-author of the new study. "What worlds can find us? How many of them and for how long?"

Lisa Kaltenegger, an astronomer at Cornell University, approached Faherty with the idea to create a map showing which nearby stars could see Earth in the past and future. "I wanted to do a billion years!" Kaltenegger says of the proposed time line. "And I was like, 'No, there's a finite clock backtrack you can do,'" Faherty explains.

The data set the two researchers used came from the Gaia mission, a spacecraft launched by the European Space Agency in 2013 to tally and track more than a billion stars throughout the Milky Way. It uses a distance-measuring technique called parallax, which can be understood by simply winking one eye, then the other and noticing how objects in your field of view shift in proportion to their proximity to you. "Your eyes are separated by a small amount of a distance, and that distance between your eyes is what allows you to measure depth," Faherty explains. That is what Gaia does, too, except its baseline is roughly the span of Earth's orbit around the sun rather than the space between a person's eyes. This longer baseline allows the spacecraft to more precisely measure celestial distances and motions. But just as with your eyeballs, there is still some uncertainty in establishing the exact kinetics of these uberdistant objects, Faherty says.

So the pair settled on a 10,000-year window stretching from 5,000 years ago to 5,000 years from now. The timeline is conservative, Faherty says, considering Earth is 4.55 billion years old. But the temporal component is still especially significant because everything in space is moving over time, says René Heller, an astrophysicist at the Max Planck Institute for Solar Systems Research in Göttingen, Germany, who was not involved with the study. "What's happening in space is dynamic–it's not a static picture!" he says.

From the Gaia data set, Faherty and Kaltenegger picked out the stars within about 300 light-years of our sun–those "in our neighborhood," Faherty says. Thanks to Gaia and other surveys, the researchers already knew how fast each star is moving, so they pushed the stars' trajectories backward and forward through time on a big virtual map. This approach allowed them to determine when and where these neighborhood stars entered, or will enter, the so-called Earth transit zone, or what Faherty calls the "bull's eye in the sky": the area where a star may be aligned just right to get a glimpse of our world crossing the face of the sun.

That is the same method astronomers here on Earth have used with great success to find and study thousands of worlds around other stars. By monitoring a star continuously, observers can seek out a regular pattern of "dimmings and rebrightenings" produced by shadowy planets parading across the star's face as seen from our solar system. This remarkable method does not just tell us if there are planets encircling a star–it also allows observers to scry the bulk chemical composition of the planet's air via starlight shining through its upper atmosphere. "When the planet passes in front of the star, it leaves a spectral fingerprint, as we call it–information about its atmosphere in the starlight," Heller says.

Kaltenegger and Faherty's study is not, it turns out, the first to look for other planetary systems that could catch Earth in transit. Heller and one of his colleagues created a similar map in 2016, although that earlier work tallied just 82 stars that would be aligned in the right position–and it did not implement the temporal component that the Gaia data set allowed Kaltenegger and Faherty to include in their new paper. "We thought about whether others might look for transiting planets as we do but from an extrasolar perspective," Heller says of his previous work. "And some of them might be lucky in seeing us earthlings transiting in front of the sun."

Looking at Earth and the solar system from this flipped perspective is extremely valuable, Kaltenegger says. "The most impressive image ever, I think, is the pale blue dot picture that Carl Sagan helped to make." In that famous photograph, captured by the outbound *Voyager 1* probe beyond the orbit of Pluto, a minuscule pinprick of light (Earth) hangs in a diagonal sunbeam against the dark void of space, its vaguely cyan color hinting at the presence of watery oceans and clouds. The image is a viscerally visual depiction of William Blake's oft-quoted musing about glimpsing "a world in a grain of sand," showing how even a single pixel of planetary light falling on some faraway detector can reveal surprising amounts of astrobiologically relevant information. The view from *Voyager 1* is a testament to the chilling, exhilarating fact that, just as we can see ourselves from the interstellar depths, others can, too.

Seven of the stars mapped by Kaltenegger and Faherty are known to host possibly rocky exoplanets thought to be passable candidates for harboring liquid water–and thus life as we know it–on their surface. One of these, the world called Ross 128 b, was in Earth's transit zone for about 2,000 years. It "saw" our planet between the 10th century BCE and the 10th century CE, a time period comprising the reign of Alexander the Great, the fall of Rome, and the zenith of the Mayan civilization. But the best known view is yet to come and exists around another star called TRAPPIST-1. This star is encircled by seven approximately Earth-sized planets. Four are at the right distance from TRAPPIST-1 to conceivably support life, Kaltenegger says. The star and its retinue of worlds will enter Earth's transit zone in about 1,600 years.

These stars and related systems should be priority one for current and future efforts to seek out exoplanets that may bear not only life but perhaps even alien technological civilizations, some astronomers say. "I would put the targets mentioned at the top of the list," says Jill Tarter, chair emeritus for research on the search for extraterrestrial life (SETI) at the SETI Institute, who was not involved with the new study.

Back on Earth, how might we prepare for when TRAPPIST-1 enters our sight line in 1,600 years—or for when any exoplanets do so, for that matter? Heller says that it is a somewhat futile exercise to make 37th-century plans with 21st-century technology. And humanity might not even be here that far into the future, an option Heller has whimsically considered for imagination's sake. We could install some sort of co-orbiting giant sign or apparatus that would imprint its shadow on the sun's outgoing light alongside our planet but would stay locked away if someone pressed a button once per year, he says. The sign would thus inflate once we were gone (or had forgotten about it) to display the message "Nice not knowing you" to any beings that came across it in our absence, he jokes.

Faherty says that beyond orienting searches for extraterrestrial life, she hopes this new star map inspires and opens minds. The project expanded how she thinks about our chances of encountering other worlds, she says. "I got an eerie feeling of ships passing in the night [doing this work]," Faherty adds. Heller says he also has a strange feeling about being contacted. "Think of living in a room, and all the windows are open, and you do all your business, and you don't know that all the windows are open," he says. "Would you behave differently if you knew that you are being seen all your life?"

About the Author

Tess Joosse was formerly an Editorial Fellow at Scientific American. *She earned a master's degree in science communication from the University of California, Santa Cruz.*

Maybe the Aliens Really Are Here

By John Gertz

SETI, as a modern astronomical endeavor, dates to 1959 (first paper) and 1960 (first observation). Modern UFO sightings date to the late 1940s. Though superficially similar, the two fields in practice have had virtually nothing to do with one another. SETI usually requires a graduate degree in astronomy, and its scientists tend to disdain UFOers for requiring nothing more than a camera that takes blurry photos and a butterfly net in case a little green man appears.

However, the two camps may be moving closer together.

In the classic SETI paradigm, stars are observed for artificial signals. But this communication strategy has severe drawbacks from ET's point of view. In order for it to succeed, ET would have to target each of potentially millions of promising nearby stars (including ours) continuously, and do so over potentially billions of years. Additionally, it would need to maintain a dedicated receiver for each target star to be certain not to miss a return message if and when it arrives. The cost of this strategy to ET in time, energy and materials would be immeasurable. Further, by announcing its presence to so many stars, it invites disaster should any civilization prove aggressive. Added to this is the problem of communicating with a target civilization of which it would know nothing. Perhaps the transmitting civilization communicates in color oscillations like a cuttlefish, while the recipient only understands bee-like waggles.

Building on the work of others, I have hypothesized that aliens would be better served by sending robotic probes. Relatively simple flyby probes might intermittently surveil nascent solar systems, for example, at 200-million-year intervals. Star systems with biogenic planets might be surveilled more often. Highly capable probes might be placed permanently in the vicinity of planets that have achieved multicellularity as indicated by their oxygen-rich atmospheres or other biosignatures.

Once a permanently placed probe had detected artificial electromagnetic leakage, indicating that one multicellular species had become technologically intelligent, it would attempt to decode the species. Using *Sesame Street*, Khan Academy, and YouTube, and even granted its enormous onboard AI capabilities, it would still take time for it to decode *Homo sapiens'* languages, science, math and culture. After many decades of work by E. O. Wilson and others, we now know a little something about ant communication but are still far from a complete decoding. How very much more difficult would it be for ET to decode humans? Even if it has been watching episodes of *I Love Lucy* that have been leaking out into space since that show was first broadcast, it may still not understand them.

The local probe might need to send data back to its home base for deeper analysis and/or instructions on how to proceed. If the probe began transmitting data to its home in 1950 after its detection of early television signals, and if that home base were located at the modest distance of 150 light-years, then the earliest year in which the probe might receive instructions to make contact with Earth would be 2250.

However, when we do finally hear from a local probe, after it has decoded us, its transmissions may be in a terrestrial language. The ensuing dialogue will take place in near real time, as opposed to the painfully slow dialogue between ourselves and an alien civilization transmitting from a star at hundreds or thousands of light-years distance. An alien probe need not reveal the location of its home base, obviating any danger to the progenitor civilization. A fully autonomous probe would be able to communicate with us even if its progenitor civilization is long extinct.

Provided that a probe does belong to an existing civilization or network of civilizations, there remains the problem of how it might communicate with them. To do so directly would require an enormous transmitter. The better solution would be to string communication nodes at close proximity to one another, perhaps one in orbit around every star, and perhaps located at a sufficient distance from the star to enable the use of it as a gravity lens, per

Einstein's theory of general relativity. For the sun, that focal point begins at 550 Earth-sun distances (AU) at which point the node would achieve signal gain of approximately a billion.

Large numbers of ET civilization might contribute to this nodal system, and the store of information would only grow with time regardless of whether the contributing civilizations persist or have gone extinct. We might contribute Aristotle, Shakespeare, Beethoven, and Monet to this Encyclopedia Galactica. However, we will not be in a position to barter our culture; having surveilled our TV and internet for at least 70 years, ET has probably already uploaded all it wants. Nonetheless, ET may wish to recruit us into the galactic club so that we might manufacture probes and nodes and otherwise take responsibility for the maintenance of the interstellar communication system within our immediate stellar neighborhood. That would be our bargaining chip.

SETI stellar observations presume a very faint signal that would require Earth's most powerful telescopes to detect. However, highly sensitive telescopes have very small fields of view. Detecting a local robotic probe requires the opposite strategy. Because of a probe's close proximity to Earth, its signal would be much brighter than an interstellar beacon, even under the conservative assumption that its transmission will be on the order of only a few watts. Consequently, SETI's best strategy would be to sacrifice great sensitivity in favor of a wide a field of view or, better yet, all-sky-all-the-time observing. Such systems are being built now or planned.

Purported sightings by military pilots of objects that defy all known aerodynamics in their sudden and steep accelerations may be delusions, hoaxes or optical illusions. Nevertheless, many SETI scientists now agree with UFOers that the first alien detection plausibly could occur within our own solar system. Both UFOers and SETI scientists should also agree that if some UFO sightings are genuine sightings of aliens, then they must be of robotic probes rather than vessels crewed by biological beings. If nothing else, such beings would be crushed by the g-forces of their purported, very large, accelerations.

The evidence is still lacking that would fully unify UFOers and SETI scientists—and yet the space between these two groups may not be so far vast after all.

This is an opinion and analysis article; the views expressed by the author or authors are not necessarily those of Scientific American.

About the Author

John Gertz is the president of the Foundation for Investing in Research on SETI Science and Technology and former Chairman of the Board of the SETI Institute. He is also president and CEO of Zorro productions, a multi-media entertainment company.

The Origin of Technosignatures

By Caleb A. Scharf

The search for extraterrestrial intelligence stands out in the quest to find life elsewhere because it assumes that certain kinds of life will manipulate and exploit its environment with intention. And that intention may go far beyond just supporting essential survival and function. By contrast, the general search for other living systems, or biosignatures, really is all about eating, reproducing, and, not to put too fine a point on it, making waste.

The assumption of intention has a long history. Back in the late 1800s and early 1900s the American astronomer Percival Lowell convinced himself, and others, of "non-natural features" on the surface of Mars and associated these with the efforts of an advanced but dying species to channel water from the polar regions. Around the same time, Nikola Tesla suggested the possibility of using wireless transmission to contact Mars, and even thought that he might have picked up repeating, structured signals from beyond the Earth. Nearly a century earlier, the great mathematician and physicist Carl Friedrich Gauss had also thought about active contact and suggested carving up the Siberian tundra to make a geometric signal that could be seen by extraterrestrials.

Today the search for intention is represented by a still-coalescing field of cosmic "technosignatures," which encompasses the search for structured electromagnetic signals as well as a wide variety of other evidence of intentional manipulation of matter and energy–from alien megastructures to industrial pollution, or nighttime lighting systems on distant worlds.

But there's a puzzle that really comes ahead of all of this. We tend to automatically assume that technology in all of the forms known to us is a marker of "advanced" life and its intentions, but we seldom ask the fundamental question of why technology happens in the first place.

I started thinking about this conundrum back in 2018, and it leads to a deeper way to quantify intelligent life, based on the external information that a species generates, utilizes, propagates, and encodes in what we call technology–everything from cave paintings and books to flash drives and cloud servers and the structures sustaining them. To give this a label I called it the "dataome." One consequence of this reframing of the nature of our world is that our quest for technosignatures is actually, in the end, about the detection of extraterrestrial dataomes.

A critical aspect of this reframing is that a dataome may be much more like a living system than any kind of isolated, inert, synthetic system. This rather provocative (well, OK, very provocative) idea is one of the conclusions I draw in a much more detailed investigation my new book *The Ascent of Information*. Our informational world, our dataome, is best thought of as a symbiotic entity to us (and to life on Earth in general). It genuinely is another "ome," not unlike the microbiomes that exist in an intimate and inextricable relationship with all multicellular life.

As such, the arrival of a dataome on a world represents an origin event. Just as the origin of biological life is, we presume, represented by the successful encoding of self-propagating, evolving information in a substrate of organic molecules. A dataome is the successful encoding of self-propagating, evolving information into a different substrate, and with a seemingly different spatial and temporal distribution–routing much of its function through a biological system like us. And like other major origin events, it involves the wholesale restructuring of the planetary environment, from the utilization of energy to fundamental chemical changes in atmospheres or oceans.

In other words, I'd claim that technosignatures are a consequence of dataomes, just as biosignatures are a consequence of genomes.

That distinction may seem subtle, but it's important. Many remotely observable biosignatures are a result of the inner chemistry of life; metabolic byproducts like oxygen or methane in planetary atmospheres for example. Others are consequences of how life harvests energy, such as the colors of pigments associated with photosynthesis. All of these signatures are deeply rooted in the genomes of life, and ultimately that's how we understand their basis and likelihood, and how we disentangle these markers from challenging and incomplete astronomical measurements.

Analogous to biosignatures, technosignatures must be rooted in the dataomes that coexist with biological life (or perhaps that had once coexisted with biological life). To understand the basis and likelihood of techosignatures we therefore need to recognize and study the nature of dataomes.

For example, a dataome and its biological symbiotes may exist in uneasy Darwinian balance, where the interests of each side are not always aligned, but coexistence provides a statistical advantage to each. This could be a key factor for evaluating observations about environmental compositions and energy transformations on other worlds. We ourselves are experiencing an increase in the carbon content of our atmosphere that can be associated with the exponential growth of our dataome, yet that compositional change is not good for preserving the conditions that our biological selves have thrived in.

Projecting where our own dataome is taking us could provide clues to the scales and qualities of technosignatures elsewhere. If we only think about technosignatures as if they're an arbitrary collection of phenomena rather than a consequence of something Darwinian in nature, it could be easy to miss what's going on out there in the cosmos.

About the Author

Caleb A. Scharf is director of astrobiology at Columbia University. He is author and co-author of more than 100 scientific research articles in astronomy and astrophysics. His work has been featured in publications such as New Scientist, Scientific American, Science News, Cosmos Magazine, Physics Today *and* National Geographic. *For many years he wrote the* Life, Unbounded *blog for* Scientific American.

Section 4: Making Contact

How to Tell if Extraterrestrial Visitors Are Friend or Foe

By Avi Loeb

Despite the naive storylines about interstellar travel in science fiction, biological creatures were not selected by Darwinian evolution to survive travel between stars. Such a trip would necessarily span many generations, since even at the speed of light, it would take tens of thousands of years to travel between stars in our galaxy's disk and 10 times longer across its halo. If we ever encounter traces of aliens, therefore, it will likely be in the form of technology, not biology. Technological debris could have accumulated in interstellar space over the past billions of years, just as plastic bottles have accumulated on the surface of the ocean. The chance of detecting alien technological relics can be simply calculated from their number per unit volume near us rather than from the Drake equation, which applies strictly to communication signals from living civilizations.

On a recent podcast about my book *Extraterrestrial*, I was asked whether extraterrestrial intelligence should be expected to follow the rational underpinning of morality, as neatly formulated by the German philosopher Immanuel Kant. This would be of concern to us during an encounter. Based on human history, I expressed doubt that morality would garner a global commitment from all intelligent beings in the Milky Way.

Instead, a code of conduct that allows systems of alien technology to dominate the galaxy would also make them more likely to be the way we would first encounter extraterrestrials. Practically, this rule will act as a sort of Darwinian evolution by natural selection, favoring systems that can persevere over long times and distances; and multiply quickly and spread at the highest speed with self-repair mechanisms that mitigate damage along their journey. Such systems could have reached the habitable zones around all stars within the Milky Way, including our sun, by now. Most stars formed billions of years before ours did, and technological equipment sent from habitable planets near them could have predated us by enough time to dominate the galaxy before we came to exist as a technological species.

Our own artificial intelligence systems are likely to supersede many features of human intelligence within the coming decade. It is therefore reasonable to imagine AI systems connected to 3-D printers that would replicate themselves on planet surfaces and adapt to changing circumstances along their journey between planets through machine learning. They could hibernate during long journeys and turn on close to stars, using starlight to recharge their energy supply. With this in mind, it is conceivable that the flat thin structure that might have characterized the interstellar object 'Oumuamua was meant to collect sunlight and recharge its batteries. The same dish could have also served as a receiver for communication signals from probes that were already deposited on habitable planets, like Earth or Mars.

And speaking about such probes–if one or more of the unidentified aerial phenomena (UAP) discussed in the Pentagon report to Congress is potentially extraterrestrial in origin, then scientists have an obligation to decipher their purpose by collecting more data on their behavior. Owing to the long time-delay of any signals from their point of origin, these objects are likely to act autonomously. How could we tell whether an autonomous extraterrestrial AI system is a friend or a foe?

Initial impressions can be misleading, as in the story of the Trojan Horse used by the Greeks to enter the city of Troy and win the Trojan War. Therefore, we should first study the behavior of alien probes to figure out what type of data they are seeking. Second, we should examine how they respond to our actions. And with no choice left, we should engage their attention in a way that would promote our interests.

But most importantly, humanity should avoid sending mixed messages to these probes, because that would confuse our interpretation of their response. Any decision on how to act must be coordinated by an international organization such as the United Nations and policed consistently by all governments on Earth. In particular, it would be prudent to appoint a forum composed of our most accomplished experts in the areas of computing (to interpret the meaning of any signal we intercept), physics (to understand the physical characteristics of the systems with which we interact), and strategy (to coordinate the best policy for accomplishing our goals).

Ultimately, we might need to employ our own AI in order to properly interpret the alien AI. The experience will be as humbling as relying on our kids to make sense of new content on the internet by admitting that their computer skills exceed ours. The quality of expertise and AI might be more important than physical strength or natural intelligence in determining the outcome of a technological battlefield.

Being the smartest species on Earth, our fate has been under our control so far. This may not hold true after our encounter with extraterrestrial AI systems. Hence, technological maturity obtains a sense of urgency for Darwinian survival in the global competition of Milky Way civilizations. Only by becoming sufficiently advanced can we overcome threats from alien technological equipment. Here's hoping that in the galactic race, our AI systems will outsmart the aliens. Just as in the gunfights of the Wild West, the survivor might be the one who is first to draw a weapon without hesitation.

This is an opinion and analysis article; the views expressed by the author or authors are not necessarily those of Scientific American.

About the Author

Avi Loeb is former chair (2011-2020) of the astronomy department at Harvard University, founding director of Harvard's Black Hole Initiative and director of the Institute for Theory and Computation at the Harvard-Smithsonian Center for Astrophysics. He also chairs the Board on Physics and Astronomy of the National Academies and the advisory board for the Breakthrough Starshot project, and is a member of President's Council of Advisors on Science and Technology. Loeb is the bestselling author of Extraterrestrial: The First Sign of Intelligent Life Beyond Earth *(Houghton Mifflin Harcourt).*

Contact: The Day After

By Tim Folger

One day last spring Frank Drake returned to the observatory at Green Bank, W.Va., to repeat a search he first conducted there in 1960 as a 30-year-old astronomer. Green Bank has the largest steerable telescope in the world–a 100-meter-wide radio dish. Drake wanted to aim it at the same two sunlike stars he had observed 50 years ago, Tau Ceti and Epsilon Eridani, each a bit more than 10 light-years from Earth, to see if he could detect radio transmissions from any civilizations that might exist on planets orbiting either of the two stars. This encore observing run was largely ceremonial for the man who pioneered the worldwide collaborative effort known as SETI–the search for extraterrestrial intelligence. As a young man, Drake had half-expected to find a cosmos humming with the equivalent of ET ham radio chatter. The elder Drake did not expect any such surprises from Tau Ceti or Epsilon Eridani. The Great Silence, as some astronomers call the absence of alien communiqués, remains unbroken after five decades of searching. And yet so does Drake's conviction that it is only a matter of time before SETI succeeds.

"Fifty years ago, when I made the first search, it took two months–200 hours of observing time at Green Bank," says Drake, who is now chairman emeritus at the SETI Institute in Mountain View, Calif. "When I went back this year, they gave me an hour to repeat the experiment. That turned out to be way too much time. It took eight tenths of a second–each star took four tenths of a second! And the search was better. I looked at the same two stars over a much wider frequency band with higher sensitivity and more channels, in eight tenths of a second. That shows how far we've come. And the rate of improvement hasn't slowed down at all."

Computer-processing power has roughly doubled every two years for the past 50. Drake and other SETI scientists believe that within 30 years or so, computing advances will allow them to sift through enough frequencies from enough of the 200 billion stars in our galaxy to have a reasonable shot at finding a signal from an extraterrestrial civilization. "My guess–and 'guess' is the right word–is that the number of detectable civilizations in our galaxy right now is 10,000," Drake says. "That means one of every some millions of stars has a detectable civilization." His estimate, he adds, assumes an average life span of about 10,000 years for a technological civilization. "In 20 or 30 years we will be able to look at 10 million stars. That's the challenge, even though it's based on a guess."

Drake may be too conservative, says Seth Shostak, senior astronomer at the SETI Institute. "If this experiment has merit, it's going to succeed within two or three decades," he says. "If it doesn't, then there's something fundamentally wrong in our assumptions. If it's going to happen, it's going to happen soon."

Drake and Shostak could, of course, be wildly off base. It is not hard to find astronomers who would peg the number of civilizations in our galaxy at one–our own. But if Drake and Shostak are right–if we are within a few decades of discovering that we are not alone in the universe–what then? What happens after we detect a signal from an alien intelligence? Could we even translate the message? How likely is it that the message might contain knowledge that would transform our culture? Would it be dangerous to respond and reveal our existence to beings from other worlds?

One thing that definitely won't happen if SETI scientists discover such a signal is a government cover-up or any sort of conspiratorial secrecy. The world will learn the news almost immediately. Shostak is certain of this. So is Jill Tarter, director of the SETI Institute's research center. They know exactly how events will unfold when they finally find a signal because on a June morning 13 years ago, they thought they had received one.

Dress Rehearsal

It happened at about 6 a.m. Tarter was at the Green Bank observatory when the signal came in. It was bunch of signals at discrete frequencies, with uniform spacing between them, which looked on a graph like a comb. "It was clearly an engineered signal," she says. Tarter and her colleagues at Green Bank followed their protocols to rule out false alarms. They swung the telescope away from the target star. The signal vanished. They aimed at the star again. The signal came back. Ordinarily they would have verified the precise origin of the signal with a separate telescope at an observatory in Woodbury, Ga. But lightning had recently struck that telescope and fried its hard drive.

"It was rural Georgia, and it took about three days to get FedEx in there with a replacement drive," Tarter says. "In the meantime, we had telescope time in West Virginia"—SETI observations typically piggyback on other, mainstream astronomical research—"and we were going to use it. Without our second site, the only thing we could do was nod back and forth between two different stars."

Tarter, who had been scheduled to fly home to California at noon that day, canceled her flight and left a phone message for Chris Neller, her assistant in Mountain View, to tell her about the change in plans. By late afternoon the target star that was thought to be the source of the signal began to set below the horizon. That is when Tarter and her team realized something was wrong. Although the target star was setting, the source of the signal seemed to be climbing, its strength undiminished. The signal, they eventually determined, was coming from a NASA satellite, the Solar and Heliospheric Observatory, or SOHO.

During all the excitement, no one remembered to call the Mountain View office to tell them the whole episode had been a false alarm. Meanwhile Ann Druyan, Carl Sagan's widow, had by chance called Mountain View to talk with Tarter about something unrelated. Neller told Druyan that Tarter was delayed at the Green Bank observatory, studying what might be a signal from an extraterrestrial civilization. Druyan immediately called William J. Broad, a science reporter for the *New York Times*. Broad in turn called Shostak to confirm the story.

"The beauty of a false alarm is that you see what really happens," Shostak says. "It's no longer theoretical. Not a false alarm that lasts five minutes, but where for the better part of a day you think, maybe this is it. You have these nifty protocols, but what really happens? People don't follow protocols. It's not that people do anything mischievous or malevolent–you're so caught up in the excitement of the moment, the media are immediately calling you on the phone, people send emails to their friends."

In the event of a signal that survives initial scrutiny–one that is quickly verified by a second observatory–the astronomers who made the discovery would send an International Astronomical Union (IAU) telegram–now delivered as an email–to observatories around the world. Astronomers use IAU telegrams to notify one another of time-sensitive observations: supernovas, comets, or gamma-ray bursts. Tarter says a SETI observation would be treated like any other astronomical discovery. "If something like that happens, we'll want everybody who can to look at it right away," she says. "We'd like people to look in the signal's direction, with different tools, checking different frequencies, and try to figure it out."

Verifying the Message

SETI scientists think they know, in broad terms, what an ET signal will look like. To stand out as obviously artificial against a background of natural cosmic radio emissions, the signal would have to be narrow, with a lot of energy packed into a few frequencies. Natural phenomena, such as pulsars and interstellar gases, spew out radio emissions at many different frequencies. If an observatory ever receives a narrowband signal coming from an astronomical distance, the source would almost certainly be artificial.

According to voluntary, nonbinding protocols adopted by SETI researchers around the world, if IAU astronomers confirmed a signal as genuine, they would then notify the United Nations and various world leaders. Tarter says that some generous SETI sponsors would also receive discreet thank-you calls. At that point the astronomers who made the discovery would be free to hold a press conference–if the story had not already been leaked. But even those modest constraints would probably be breached. "The protocols are just a nice idea," Shostak says. "They're like red lights in Naples, Italy," he laughs. "They're suggestions."

What happens next? A triumphant announcement, followed by headlines? Panic? New Age celebrations of galactic harmony? Probably none of the above, except for the headlines, if Douglas Vakoch is right. A psychologist by training, Vakoch has an office across the hall from Tarter at the SETI Institute and must have the world's most unusual job title: director of interstellar message composition.

"While we may be able to detect that there is a signal that at least initially appears distinctly artificial, I suspect even that claim would be questioned," Vakoch says. "There would be a lot of people trying to come up with natural explanations. I think the assumption that one day someone is going to announce that we've discovered extraterrestrial intelligence, and now the world knows, is a fallacy, because there's going to be much more ambiguity in the process. It might be similar to what was recently considered a plausible claim that there was evidence of fossils in Martian meteorites–interesting enough to consider, but now let's look at this over the next few months."

Even if the signal is confirmed as an authentic transmission from an extraterrestrial civilization, it is unlikely that astronomers would be able to extract any information from it for many years. SETI's instruments are designed to search for steady, periodic narrowband radio pulses–carrier waves powerful enough to be detectable across many light-years. The pulse itself would yield no information, other than its artificial nature. Any message content would likely be in the form of changes in amplitude or frequency buried within the pulse. Even a large radio telescope would need to repeatedly scan a small patch of sky to build up the signal pulse above background radio noise. In doing so, it would average out modulations on finer time-scales that might contain a message. Resolving the message would require an antenna far more powerful than Earth's largest, the 305-meter dish at Arecibo, Puerto Rico.

"You would need something on the order of 10,000 times bigger than Arecibo," Shostak says. Rather than a single enormous dish, such a telescope would probably consist of many smaller antennas spread across a large area and linked electronically. Constructing such an instrument would require international collaboration and funding, with no guarantee that the message–if the signal contained one–could ever be deciphered. "That's not something you'd do overnight," Shostak observes. "That's a big project. I think we would do it, because–gosh darn it–we would want to know what they're saying."

The Fallout

Taking into account political debates and the time needed to build a telescope sensitive enough to analyze the signal, years would pass before astronomers or cryptographers could begin to attempt to decipher a message from the stars. So whereas that first contact with another intelligence would in itself be one of the most important scientific discoveries of all time, the lack of any further knowledge about the nature of that alien intelligence would limit the immediate cultural impact. The story of the discovery would monopolize headlines for a while, but our collective attention span would inevitably move on while scientists sought to translate the message.

"I have no doubt that the receipt of such a message would be a huge and genuinely exciting moment," says Charles T. Rubin, a political philosopher at Duquesne University who studies the social issues raised by SETI research. "But I don't think it would cause a great cultural shift, because the notion of extraterrestrials is common both in popular culture and in scientific circles. It would confirm what many already suspect to be true."

If some nation or group of nations decides to build an instrument that would give us a shot at cracking an extraterrestrial message, how likely is it that we would succeed? Sagan, an early advocate of SETI, imagined that we might receive an Encyclopedia Galactica, filled with the accumulated wisdom of many advanced extraterrestrial civilizations. Some SETI researchers assumed–and still assume–that the language of science might provide common ground for communication. Kathryn Denning, an anthropologist at York University in Toronto and a member of the SETI Post-Detection Taskgroup, is less sanguine.

"We run into an irreducible problem with communication that isn't face to face, and that is the problem of establishing a referent," Denning says. "If you and I speak different languages, and we're in the same room, I can point to a table, and I can say 'table,' and you infer that 'table' is my word for that thing, and then we can go from there. That's the time-honored way of learning languages. If you're not in direct contact, if you can't do that kind of pointing exercise, there's always this question of what you're referring to in these initial communications. Scientists–physical scientists and mathematicians in particular–tend to be more prone to thinking that because we'll be dealing with the same physical structures in the universe, we can use those as our Rosetta Stone, so to speak, and build up from there–send each other the value of pi, and then we're off to the races. But anthropologists tend not to be so comfortable with that. Errors can take place right at the get-go. For example, if I give you a signal–beep, beep, beep–is that three or two? Are we counting the beeps or the spaces? We have fundamental assumptions built in."

John R. Elliott, a researcher at Leeds Metropolitan University in England who studies artificial intelligence and the structure of languages, is already preparing for the day we receive the first extraterrestrial message. Even if it proves impossible to directly translate the message, it might be possible to discover patterns that Elliott suspects are fundamental to all languages. Those patterns might reveal something about the nature of the beings who sent the message, particularly how their level of intelligence compares with our own.

Elliott has devised a computer program that compares any unknown language with a database of 60 human languages. All languages, he says, share what he calls functional elements–words such as "if," "and," and "but"–that break up the complexity of a language into manageable chunks. The length of those chunks–the nouns, verbs and other words contained between the functional elements–provides a measure of our cognitive abilities. "It opens a window on our way of embedding information, the way we structure our sentences," Elliott notes. "It shows the constraints on us as intelligent authors."

Elliott says his computer program shows that the functional elements in all human languages are typically separated by no more than about nine words. Assuming an ET signal arrives as a binary stream of ones and zeros, his program would search for patterns in the message and attempt to identify the occurrence of functional elements. The program would, ideally, give us a rough measure of alien IQ by comparing the average interval between our ifs, ands, and buts with theirs. "Anything above 10 means it would exceed human cognition," he says. Elliott thinks he could determine whether a signal bears the characteristics of a language within a few days; he might be able to tell if it contains images. "For the semantic side? We might never interpret it."

Worth the Risk?

Some SETI proponents suggest we should do more than passively wait for a signal. They believe we should transmit messages and let anyone who might be listening know that we are here. Last spring, in a Discovery Channel series, Stephen Hawking of the University of Cambridge said that transmitting messages without knowing what is out there could be dangerous. He warned of the possibility of predatory aliens ravaging the resources of world after world. "If aliens visit us," he said, "the outcome would be much as when Columbus landed in America, which didn't turn out well for the Native Americans."

The SETI community seems to be divided about the wisdom of sending messages versus quietly biding our time. But in any case, it is probably too late. Radio and television signals have been leaking from our planet for decades now. "*I Love Lucy* has already passed 10,000 stars," says Dan Wertheimer, a SETI researcher at the University of California, Berkeley, who helped to develop the SETI@Home project, which allows anyone to download software to a home computer to help process SETI data. Moreover, there is no reason why an extraterrestrial civilization couldn't spot Earth using the same–or better–techniques that terrestrial astronomers are already using to find planets around other stars. Geoffrey W. Marcy, an astronomer at Berkeley who has played a leading role in the discovery of dozens of extrasolar planets, says that by the end of this century, space-based telescopes will enable us to map the continents and oceans of these worlds. And if we will soon be doing that, it is likely that extraterrestrial civilizations–if any exist–are doing it, too.

"Aliens who have a mere 1,000-year head start on us could listen to our conversation right now," Marcy says. "They could read our lips. So this passive versus active thing makes no sense to me. We can't hide–that's crazy! Any more than ants can hide from us humans. It would be like one ant talking to another ant, 'Oh, we'd better not talk because the humans would know we're here, and they might step on us.' No, sorry, guys, you ants can't hide from us!"

Drake believes Hawking's fears are unfounded, largely because interstellar travel may be practically impossible, which he believes also answers the Fermi paradox, named for Enrico Fermi, the Italian physicist who first posed it: If extraterrestrial civilizations exist, why haven't we seen them yet? Given the age of the galaxy, and its 200 billion stars, surely at least one civilization should have colonized the galaxy by now. Drake demurs.

"To give you an idea why even a very small mission won't work, just imagine a spacecraft the size of a 737 airplane, with perhaps 50 passengers. Suppose the nearest star with a habitable planet is only 10 light-years away, which is quite close–there are only a few stars that close. And assume you can go 10 percent the speed of light. Why that number? It never gets mentioned in all these discussions about space travel, but if you're going a little faster than that, about 12 percent the speed of light, if you impact a pebble, the energy in that impact is equal to what that same mass would release if it was used in a nuclear fusion bomb. It would blow up the spacecraft. One pebble in the whole trip ends the mission." But Drake believes that SETI's limited funds should go to searching, not broadcasting.

Marcy says the Fermi paradox presents a genuine problem for SETI researchers, and he sees only three possible solutions. "The fact that aliens haven't landed tells you they're rare, or that space travel is very hard, or that it's not just worth doing."

Perhaps Hawking's fears say more about us than about any aliens we might encounter. Given the history of our own species, who would have more to fear from contact, humans or extraterrestrials? SETI, unavoidably, reflects our own dreams and night terrors about our place in the universe. In postulating the presence of civilizations on other worlds, we are extrapolating wildly from a single known example–our own fragile, remarkable existence.

Realistically, though, the quest to make contact will be an endeavor that spans centuries–if our own civilization lasts that long. SETI is, perhaps, the strangest and most profound experiment in the history of our world. One of the founding fathers of SETI, the late Philip Morrison, a physicist at the Massachusetts Institute of Technology, likened the SETI project to the medieval and Renaissance recovery of the knowledge of classical antiquity, in which scholars labored for generations. The patient transcribing of ancient texts revealed a world that had been lost and eventually transformed the world the scholars thought they knew.

One day we may learn that we are not alone and, indeed, that intelligence is common in the universe. "If SETI succeeds, then intelligence happened in at least one other place," Shostak says. "So it probably happened in lots of places. In astronomy, the only numbers are one, two and infinity. So if you get two, there are probably lots more. It's like finding two elephants."

About the Author

Tim Folger has been writing about science for more than 20 years. In 2007 he won the American Institute of Physics science writing award. His work has appeared in Discover, National Geographic, Science *and other national publications.*

How Scientists Could Tell the World if They Find Alien Life

By Jonathan O'Callaghan

Relatively soon, some prominent astrobiologists say, we will most likely have either found compelling evidence for extraterrestrial life or banished its possible existence to the ever-shrinking edges of the cosmos beyond the rapidly expanding reach of our observations. Such answers could come by the end of the 2030s from any of a number of initiatives ardently seeking alien life. By then, samples from Mars will have arrived back on Earth, perhaps containing concrete proof the Red Planet once harbored organisms or still does today. Spacecraft at Jupiter's Europa and Saturn's Titan will be scouring both moons for signs of life residing in each world's subsurface ocean or, in the case of Titan, on the surface itself. And advanced telescopes on the ground and in space should be probing the atmospheres of potentially habitable exoplanets around nearby stars, looking for any that share the same biology-infused cocktail of gases as our own living Earth.

As confident as astrobiologists may be that their quest will soon bear fruit, however, they are far less certain of how to communicate that success if and when it occurs. How should they go about informing the world that we are truly not alone in this universe–especially given their field's long, troubled history of dubious claims and false alarms? They have been fooled before, after all.

Last month in the journal *Nature*, a group of scientists came to grips with the problem. Led by NASA's chief scientist James Green, the group proposed a new framework to help verify and then communicate the detection of biosignatures beyond Earth like the Torino scale for assessing the danger of asteroids. Their idea is to use a scale, from level 1 to level 7, that will allow confidence in any given case to be gradually increased. Known as the "confidence of life detection," or CoLD, scale, its initial steps would merely reflect confirmations that a result is not linked to contamination or some obviously abiotic origin, whereas its final levels would represent robust follow-up observations solidifying a link to life. "These things are complex," Green says. "But we really need to be able to communicate it simply."

There is no shortage of cautionary tales from previous efforts to publicize apparent breakthroughs. In 1996 President Bill Clinton heralded the discovery of a meteorite from Mars, ALH84001, that appeared to contain signs of life. "If this discovery is confirmed, it will surely be one of the most stunning insights into our universe that science has ever uncovered," he said in a speech at the White House. The finding was not confirmed: later analysis poured cold water on the tentative evidence of Martian life. Luckily astrobiology's positive public perception emerged relatively unscathed. Yet a repeat of that incident could now have disastrous consequences. "Today we have social media, so rumors, innuendo and purposely false information propagates like wildfire," says former NASA chief historian Steven Dick. "[It's] all the more reason to communicate effectively."

More recently, the supposed detection on Venus of atmospheric phosphine, a possible biosignature gas, had many suggesting a biological origin, but that detection has itself since been called into question. More outlandish ideas, such as the suggestion that the interstellar object 'Oumuamua found in our solar system in 2017 may have been an alien spacecraft rather than an asteroid or comet, have been met with widespread disdain from scientists and have the potential to dampen confidence in genuine detections of life. The CoLD scale could prevent scientists from "crying wolf" in this manner, Green says, because any overly cavalier claims would not pass the more stringent tests required to progress up the scale. "Life detection measurements can be sensationalized," he says.

Deciding how to approach actual detections of biosignatures is a topic other scientists have been considering, too. In July scientists met virtually at the Standards of Evidence for Life Detection workshop, led by NASA's Network for Life Detection (NfoLD) and Nexus for Exoplanet System Science (NExSS), to discuss the idea of establishing a framework much like CoLD. Hundreds of scientists took part, with many in favor of more rigorous communications protocols. "The potential for us to actually have some sort of interesting life detection event on another world is becoming greater," says the workshop's cochair Heather Graham of NASA's Goddard Space Flight Center. "We want to get ahead of that."

If scientists were to adopt the CoLD scale, the first of its be seven steps, or levels, would be the actual detection of a potential biosignature. Next, scientists would need to rule out contamination before demonstrating how the signal could be biological in origin. Nonbiological sources would then need to be ruled out, followed by an independent additional detection of a similar biosignature. Further observations would need to rule out nonbiological ideas before, finally, follow-up observations showed other examples of biological activity in the same environment, making a detection a level 7—essentially, proof of alien life.

Part of the hope is that the scientific community at large would agree to use such a scale. Agencies such as NASA might also agree to do so, which would also help dictate future missions. "If we're stuck at level 4, and we think we can go to level 6 with a mission, I want to fund that," Green says. Ultimately, once use of a scale like CoLD became ubiquitous, reviewers of journal papers could require authors to include it in any claim of biosignature detection. "One of the things we discussed at the workshop was: How do we incentivize people to use this?" says Victoria Meadows of the University of Washington, who was the workshop's other cochair. "The bottom line is that if we don't have such a scale, then people won't use it."

The call for such a step-based approach is driven by the unescapable likelihood that any initial detection of alien life is likely to be ambiguous rather than a smoking gun: any glaringly obvious indication of alien life would have been clear by now, decades into the hunt. So more subtle searches based on circumstantial evidence are coming to the fore. In October, for example, Zoë Havlena, a Ph.D. student at the New Mexico Institute of Mining and Technology, was part of a NASA-funded team that traveled to cave walls in Italy's

Apennine Mountains to collect and study samples of a mineral called gypsum, which is sometimes associated with biological activity and may be present on Mars. "[Gypsum on Mars] may be similar to what we're seeing in these cave systems," Havlena says.

Elsewhere on Mars, NASA's Perseverance rover is collecting rocky samples to return to Earth in the early 2030s that may contain evidence of life. Its first cache, however, was actually a sniff of the Martian atmosphere, Green says, to tease out whether or not the thin air around the rover contained methane. Previous missions–as well as telescopes on Earth–have found evidence for occasional bursts of the gas suffusing Mars's atmosphere. On our planet, methane is replenished by biological activity, and Perseverance's samples could reveal if the same is true on Mars. Currently on the CoLD scale, methane on Mars would rank at "about a [level] 4," Green says. But if Perseverance's sample is found to contain not only methane but methane rich in an isotope called carbon 12, that could change. "Life loves carbon 12," Green says. "If all the methane in this tube is carbon 12, we just increased our CoLD level by one." The next step would be to fly across the surface–with a drone like Perseverance's *Ingenuity* but bigger–to localize the methane to a source that could be directly investigated.

Outside of Mars, both Europa and Titan are promising locations to look for life because of their extensive subsurface oceans and, in the case of the latter, a thick atmosphere and lakes of liquid hydrocarbons. But any evidence found at the two moons is also likely to require careful analysis. Europa will be studied by NASA's *Europa Clipper's* mission from 2030 and the European Space Agency's (ESA's) Jupiter Icy Moons Explorer (JUICE) mission in 2031, while Titan will play host to a robotic drone–part of NASA's Dragonfly mission–by the mid-2030s. Madeline Garner, a graduate student at Montana State University, is currently investigating whether an instrument could be designed for robotic spaceflight that could identify the existence of DNA and RNA on these and other alien worlds. "Currently there's no known abiotic source" for DNA and RNA, Garner says. Her research into solid-state nanopore technology, currently used on the International Space Station to sequence DNA, could provide a conclusive detection capability for space probes. "If we find DNA or RNA, we know that's life," she says.

Beyond our solar system, scientists are preparing for a new era of exoplanet studies that could reveal tentative evidence for life on other worlds. At ESA, work is afoot on the Planetary Transits and Oscillations of Stars (PLATO) mission–set to launch in 2026–which will seek to find elusive Earth-like worlds orbiting sunlike stars. "We don't have a clear detection of a rocky planet in the so-called habitable zone of a solarlike star," says Heike Rauer, head of the Institute of Planetary Research at the German Aerospace Center. PLATO will aim to address that. "The best case will be a real Earth twin: a planet like Earth's mass and size the same distance from a star like our sun," Rauer says.

If or when such worlds are found, sophisticated orbital observatories currently being discussed–beyond the realm of NASA's James Webb Space Telescope, scheduled to launch this December–could lavish them with deeper scrutiny. Such telescopes could include a multibillion-dollar project now being considered by NASA, perhaps launching in the 2040s, that could directly image Earth-like planets around sunlike stars, crudely sniffing their atmospheres for signs of habitability and life and even mapping their surfaces. "We could see when the oceans are underneath us versus the continents and potentially a forest signature on the land surfaces," says Shawn Domagal-Goldman, acting deputy director of the Sciences and Exploration Directorate at NASA's Goddard Space Flight Center. If some verdant aqueous world also displayed biosignature gases such as oxygen and methane, many researchers would be convinced their long search for life had been successful. "It would be very difficult to observe a planet with the composition of Earth's atmosphere and figure out ways for nonlife processes to produce that," says Giada Arney, an exoplanet scientist at Goddard.

A framework like CoLD could go a long way to helping anyone, from scientists to journalists to the general public, assess how excited to be about such detections. But not everyone is convinced by the idea. Caleb Scharf, director of astrobiology at Columbia University, doubts that researchers could control the narrative and is uncertain whether the public would comprehend the carefully constructed messaging. "I question whether or not the scientific community is really in control of that," he says. "Just look at the last 20 months with COVID, where time and time again, we've been presented with statistics and probabilities, and we're all horrible at interpreting that stuff."

What is certain, though, is that things are progressing apace. "We're in a very different situation than even 10 years ago," Scharf says. Research across a range of fields, from examining caves on Earth to visiting distant worlds, is on the cusp of bringing us closer to the discovery (or continued refutation) of alien life than ever before. Deciding how to communicate such a thing to the world, whether through a framework like the CoLD scale or otherwise, is something that may well be worth discussing sooner rather than later. "It feels like we're not alone," says Graham Lau, an astrobiologist at the Blue Marble Space Institute of Science in Seattle. "If there is life out there, we must be close right now."

About the Author

Jonathan O'Callaghan is a freelance journalist covering commercial spaceflight, space exploration and astrophysics.

What We Can Learn from Studying UFOs

By Avi Loeb

In his book *Childhood's End*, Arthur C. Clarke tells a story of a peaceful alien invasion of Earth that comes at the expense of humanity's unique identity and culture. A report to Congress from the Pentagon and various intelligence agencies about sightings of unidentified flying objects (UFOs) by military personnel is scheduled to be made public shortly. The report reportedly concludes that some of the UFOs are likely real objects whose nature cannot be assessed with any confidence.

Most likely, the reported objects have mundane explanations, but we need better evidence to be sure. If they do represent alien technology, UFOs could potentially be robotic–autonomous equipment that follows a blueprint crafted by an intelligent species beyond Earth. They might even be self-replicating machines, as envisioned by the polymath John von Neumann.

Our current technology evolves exponentially on a timescale of a few years. The devices we use today would have seemed impossible a century ago. (Clarke is famously known for the statement that "any sufficiently advancedtechnology is indistinguishable from magic.") Global Wi-Fi connectivity and the internet revolutionized human behavior in recent decades, and so will artificial intelligence, robotics and genetic engineering in future decades. Since most stars formed billions of years before the sun, it is conceivable that technological civilizations that emerged around them had more time to develop their science and technology than we did, and created equipment that represents our future and would appear magical to us now. This hardware could be so advanced that it would look to us as an approximation to God. When such equipment visits us, the encounter would echo our childhood experience of not fully understanding the actions of a higher power looking over our shoulders.

The possibility that the Pentagon UFOs are human made can potentially be excluded by identifying behavior that cannot be reproduced by our most advanced equipment. We know our technological limits because any advance that goes well beyond them would have introduced major commercial or military benefits and would have been represented in the consumer market or on the battlefield.

Nevertheless, most people might choose to ignore the Pentagon report and maintain an attitude of business as usual. My daughter told me explicitly that she will not miss her routine soccer match on the day that the report is made public, irrespective of its content. At a recent forum about my popular-level book *Extraterrestrial* and new textbook *Life in the Cosmos*, I was asked how long humans could ignore extraterrestrial intelligent life. I replied: "Humans may choose to remain ignorant forever. They can refuse to recognize a reality that does not flatter their ego, like the simple idea that we are not the smartest species that in the Milky Way."

But reality does not care whether we ignore it or not. The existence of neighbors is not altered if we close the curtains on our windows and disregard them. The Pentagon has access to much more data than it releases to the public. Its report is expected to say that the reality of some UFOs is beyond doubt but that their nature requires further study. It is therefore an opportune time for the scientific community to take a closer look at UFOs by collecting and analyzing new data with the finest instruments and computers in a controlled setup. The new data can be obtained by measurement devices with capabilities far exceeding the equipment that provided past UFO data.

A fresh scientific study that offers reproducible evidence for UFO sightings and resolves their nature would demonstrate the power of science in answering a question that is clearly of great interest to the public. Finding a conclusive answer on the basis of open data will enhance the public's confidence in evidence-based knowledge. Currently, the UFO mystery surrounding the expected inconclusive interpretation of the Pentagon report will fuel unsubstantiated speculations. A decisive scientific experiment holds the promise of clearing up the fog.

The required instrumentation will likely involve state-of-the-art cameras on wide-field telescopes that scan the sky. The data stream would be processed by an advanced computer system that will store only the essential variable features. The focus on near-field aerial phenomena that move fast across the sky is different from astronomical surveys of distant sources, such as the upcoming Legacy Survey of Space and Time (LSST) on the Vera C. Rubin Observatory.

Irrespective of whether the origin of UFOs is terrestrial or extraterrestrial, we will learn something new and exciting from studying them scientifically. And it is not just the hardware that will interest us. It is the meaning behind its existence–the intent of those who manufactured it. A single UFO of extraterrestrial origin will inspire fear among humans that the aliens could be malevolent, as Stephen Hawking believed–but they could be benevolent as well. As in *Childhood's End*, they could be to us as nurturing parents are to young children. Here's hoping that if and when the time comes, we will learn that their intent is wise and well-meaning.

This is an opinion and analysis article; the views expressed by the author or authors are not necessarily those of Scientific American

About the Author

Avi Loeb is former chair (2011-2020) of the astronomy department at Harvard University, founding director of Harvard's Black Hole Initiative and director of the Institute for Theory and Computation at the Harvard-Smithsonian Center for Astrophysics. He also chairs the Board on Physics and Astronomy of the National Academies and the advisory board for the Breakthrough Starshot project, and is a member of President's Council of Advisors on Science and Technology. Loeb is the bestselling author of Extraterrestrial: The First Sign of Intelligent Life Beyond Earth *(Houghton Mifflin Harcourt).*

Researchers Made a New Message for Extraterrestrials

By Daniel Oberhaus

Upon discovering the existence of intelligent life beyond Earth, the first question we are most likely to ask is "How can we communicate?" As we approach the 50th anniversary of the 1974 Arecibo message–humanity's first attempt to send out a missive capable of being understood by extraterrestrial intelligence–the question feels more urgent than ever. Advances in remote sensing technologies have revealed that the vast majority of stars in our galaxy host planets and that many of these exoplanets appear capable of hosting liquid water on their surface–a prerequisite for life as we know it. The odds that at least one of these billions of planets has produced intelligent life seem favorable enough to spend some time figuring out how to say "hello."

In early March an international team of researchers led by Jonathan Jiang of NASA's Jet Propulsion Laboratory posted a paper on the preprint server arXiv.org that detailed a new design for a message intended for extraterrestrial recipients. The 13-page epistle, referred to as the "Beacon in the Galaxy," is meant to be a basic introduction to mathematics, chemistry, and biology that draws heavily on the design of the Arecibo message and other past attempts at contacting extraterrestrials. The researchers included a detailed plan for the best time of year to broadcast the message and proposed a dense ring of stars near the center of our galaxy as a promising destination. Importantly, the transmission also features a freshly designed return address that will help any alien listeners pinpoint our location in the galaxy so they can–hopefully–kick off an interstellar conversation.

"The motivation for the design was to deliver the maximum amount of information about our society and the human species in the minimal amount of message," Jiang says. "With improvements in digital technology, we can do much better than the [Arecibo message] in 1974."

Message Basics

Every interstellar message must address two fundamental questions: what to say and how to say it. Nearly all the messages that humans have broadcast into space so far start by establishing common ground with a basic lesson in science and mathematics, two topics that are presumably familiar to both ourselves and extraterrestrials. If a civilization beyond our planet is capable of building a radio telescope to receive our message, it probably knows a thing or two about physics. A far messier question is how to encode these concepts into the communiqué. Human languages are out of the question for obvious reasons, but so are our numeral systems. Though the concept of numbers is nearly universal, the way we depict them as numerals is entirely arbitrary. This is why many attempts, including "Beacon in the Galaxy," opt to design their letter as a bitmap, a way to use binary code to create a pixelated image.

The bitmap design philosophy for interstellar communication stretches back to the Arecibo message. It is a logical approach–the on/off, present/absent nature of a binary seems like it would be recognized by any intelligent species. But the strategy is not without its shortcomings. When pioneering search for extraterrestrial intelligence (SETI) scientist Frank Drake designed a prototype of the Arecibo message, he sent the binary message by post to some colleagues, including several Nobel laureates. None of them were able to understand its contents, and only one figured out that the binary was meant to be a bitmap. If some of the smartest humans struggle to understand this form of encoding a message, it seems unlikely that an extraterrestrial would fare any better. Furthermore, it is not even clear that space aliens will be able to see the images contained within the message if they do receive it.

"One of the key ideas is that, because vision has evolved independently many times on Earth, that means aliens will have it, too," says Douglas Vakoch, president of METI (Messaging Extraterrestrial Intelligence) International, a nonprofit devoted to researching how to communicate with other life-forms. "But that's a big 'if,' and even if they can see, there is so much culture embedded in the way we represent objects. Does that mean we should rule out pictures? Absolutely not. It means we should not naively assume that our representations are going to be intelligible."

In 2017 Vakoch and his colleagues sent the first interstellar message transmitting scientific information since 2003 to a nearby star. It, too, was coded in binary, but it eschewed bitmaps for a message design that explored the concepts of time and radio waves by referring back to the radio wave carrying the message. Jiang and his colleagues chose another path. They based much of their design on the 2003 Cosmic Call broadcast from the Yevpatoriaradio telescope in the region of Crimea. This message featured a custom bitmap "alphabet" created by physicists Yvan Dutil and Stéphane Dumas as a protoalien language that was designed to be robust against transmission errors.

After an initial transmission of a prime number to mark the message as artificial, Jiang's message uses the same alien alphabet to introduce our base-10 numeral system and basic mathematics. With this foundation in place, the message uses the spin-flip transition of a hydrogen atom to explain the idea of time and mark when the transmission was sent from Earth, introduce common elements from the periodic table, and reveal the structure and chemistry of DNA. The final pages are probably the most interesting to extraterrestrials but also the least likely to be understood because they assume that the recipient represents objects in the same way that humans do. These pages feature a sketch of a male and female human, a map of Earth's surface, a diagram of our solar system, the radio frequency that the extraterrestrials should use to respond to the message, and the coordinates of our solar system in the galaxy referenced to the location of globular clusters–stable and tightly packed groups of thousands of stars that would likely be familiar to an extraterrestrial anywhere in the galaxy.

"We know the location of more than 50 globular clusters," Jiang says. "If there's an advanced civilization, we bet that, if they know astrophysics, they know the globular cluster locations as well, so we can use this as a coordinate to pinpoint the location of our solar system."

To Send Or Not?

Jiang and his colleagues propose sending their message from either the Allen Telescope Array in northern California or the Five-Hundred-Meter Aperture Spherical Radio Telescope (FAST) in China. Since the recent destruction of the Arecibo telescope in Puerto Rico, these two radio telescopes are the only ones in the world that are actively courting SETI researchers. At the moment, though, both telescopes are only capable of listening to the cosmos, not talking to it. Jiang acknowledges that outfitting either telescope with the equipment required to transmit the message will not be trivial. But doing so is possible, and he says he and his co-authors are discussing ways to work with researchers at FAST to make it happen.*

If Jiang and his colleagues get a chance to transmit their message, they calculated that it would be best to do so sometime in March or October, when Earth is at a 90-degree angle between the sun and its target at the center of the Milky Way. This would maximize the chance that the missive would not get lost in the background noise of our host star. But a far deeper question is whether we should be sending a message at all.

Messaging extraterrestrials has always occupied a controversial position in the broader SETI community, which is mostly focused on listening for alien transmissions rather than sending out our own. To detractors of "active SETI," the practice is a waste of time at best and an existentially dangerous gamble at worst. There are billions of targets to choose from, and the odds that we send a message to the right planet at the right time are dismally low.

Plus, we have no idea who may be listening. What if we give our address to an alien species that lives on a diet of bipedal hominins?

"I don't live in fear of an invading horde, but other people do. And just because I don't share their fear doesn't make their concerns irrelevant," says Sheri Wells-Jensen, an associate professor of English at Bowling Green State University and an expert on the linguistic and cultural issues associated with interstellar message design. "Just because it would be difficult to achieve global consensus on what to send or whether we should send doesn't mean we shouldn't do it. It is our responsibility to struggle with this and include as many people as possible."

Despite the pitfalls, many insist that the potential rewards of active SETI far outweigh the risks. First contact would be one of the most momentous occasions in the history of our species, the argument goes, and if we just wait around for someone to call us, it may never happen. As for the risk of annihilation by a malevolent space alien: we blew our cover long ago. Any extraterrestrial capable of traveling to Earth would be more than capable of detecting evidence of life in the chemical signatures of our atmosphere or the electromagnetic radiation that has been leaking from our radios, televisions and radar systems for the past century. "This is an invitation to all people on Earth to participate in a discussion about sending out this message," Jiang says. "We hope, by publishing this paper, we can encourage people to think about this."

**Editor's Note (4/11/22): This sentence was edited after posting to indicate that the authors of the new paper are discussing how they might be able to use the FAST telescope but are not in direct contact with researchers there.*

About the Author

Daniel Oberhaus is a science writer based in Brooklyn, N.Y. He was previously a staff writer at Wired *covering space exploration and the future of energy. His first book,* Extraterrestrial Languages *(MIT Press, 2019), is about the art and science of interstellar communication.*

GLOSSARY

abiotic Not derived from living organisms.

astrobiology A scientific field that studies the origins, evolution, distribution, and future of life in the universe.

autonomous Having the freedom to control one's own affairs.

biogenesis The development of life from preexisting life.

biosignature Something that indicates the presence life.

cognition The mental process of acquiring knowledge and understanding through thought, experience, and the senses.

extremophile Organism that lives under extreme environmental conditions.

nucleotide Any of several compounds that are the basic structural units of RNA and DNA.

paradox A statement that is seemingly contradictory or opposed to common sense and yet is possibly true.

primordial Existing at or from the beginning of time.

Proxima Centauri A small star located in the constellation of Centaurus and the nearest star to the sun.

sanguine Optimistic or hopeful, especially in a difficult situation.

semantic Relating to meaning in language.

technosignature Any measurable effect that provides scientific evidence of past or present technology.

FURTHER INFORMATION

Croswell, Ken. "Alien Life Prefers Circles," *Scientific American*, March 1, 2015, https://www.scientificamerican.com/article/alien-life-prefers-circles/

Davis, Jason. "Is There Anybody out There?" The Planetary Society, October 25, 2017, https://www.planetary.org/articles/20171025-seti-anybody-out-there

Frank, Adam. "A new frontier is opening in the search for extraterrestrial life," *The Washington Post*, December 31, 2020, https://www.washingtonpost.com/outlook/2020/12/31/breakthrough-listen-seti-technosignatures/

Gritz, Jennie Rothenberg. "The Wonder of Avi Loeb," *Smithsonian Magazine*, October 2021, https://www.smithsonianmag.com/science-nature/wonder-avi-loeb-180978579/

McGreevy, Nora. "Balancing Homework and A.P. Classes, These High Schoolers Discovered Four Exoplanets," *Smithsonian Magazine*, February 1, 2021, https://www.smithsonianmag.com/smithsonian-institution/high-schoolers-discovered-four-exoplanets-smithsonian-180976884/

Scoles, Sarah. "'Dr. Phosphine' and the Possibility of Life on Venus," *Wired*, September 14, 2020, https://www.wired.com/story/dr-phosphine-and-the-possibility-of-life-on-venus/

Shostak, Seth. "Harvard's Avi Loeb Thinks We Should Study UFOs–and He's Not Wrong," *Scientific American*, July 29, 2021, https://www.scientificamerican.com/article/harvard-rsquo-s-avi-loeb-thinks-we-should-study-ufos-mdash-and-he-rsquo-s-not-wrong/

Wall, Mike. "The search for alien life," Space, July 19, 2021, https://www.space.com/alien-life-search.html

CITATIONS

1.1 When Did Life Start in the Universe? by Avi Loeb (November 24, 2021); 1.2 Did Life Come from Another World? by David Warmflash and Benjamin Weiss (November 1, 2005); 1.3 Origin of Life on Earth by Alonso Ricardo and Jack W. Szostak (September 1, 2009); 1.4 Looking for Life in the Multiverse by Alejandro Jenkins and Gilad Perez (January 1, 2010); 1.5 Our Improbable Existence Is No Evidence for a Multiverse by Philip Goff (January 10, 2021); 1.6 Are Aliens among Us? by Paul Davies (December 1, 2007); 2.1 Life Is Complicated—Literally, Astrobiologists Say by Natalie Elliot (November 23, 2021); 2.2 Hardy Microbes Hint at Possibilities for Extraterrestrial Life by Brianne Palmer (July 21, 2021); 2.3 How to Search for Life on Mars by Christopher P. McKay and Victor Parro García (June 1, 2014); 2.4 New Approach Could Boost the Search for Life in Otherworldly Oceans by Natalie Elliot (July 16, 2021); 2.5 Hunt for Alien Life Tops Next-Gen Wish List for U.S. Astronomy by Lee Billings (November 4, 2021); 2.6 How to Search for Life as We Don't Know It by Avi Loeb (September 26, 2021); 3.1 Alone in a Crowded Milky Way by Caleb Scharf (January 1, 2020); 3.2 If There Are Aliens Out There, Where Are They? by Mario Livio and Joe Silk (January 6, 2016); 3.3 Alien Hunters Discover Mysterious Signal from Proxima Centauri by Jonathan O'Callaghan and Lee Billings (December 18, 2020); 3.4 Aliens Might Already Be Watching Us by Tess Joosse (July 1, 2021); 3.5 Maybe the Aliens Really Are Here by John Gertz (June 21, 2021); 3.6 The Origin of Technosignatures by Caleb A. Scharf (July 2, 2021); 4.1 How to Tell if Extraterrestrial Visitors Are Friend or Foe by Avi Loeb (July 12, 2021); 4.2 Contact: The Day After by Tim Folger (January 1, 2011); 4.3 How Scientists Could Tell the World if They Find Alien Life by Jonathan O'Callaghan (November 10, 2021); 4.4 What We Can Learn from Studying UFOs by Avi Loeb (June 24, 2021); 4.5 Researchers Made a New Message for Extraterrestrials by Daniel Oberhaus (March 30, 2022)

INDEX